"You lookin' to visit someone?"

"I sure am," Clint replied. "Sean Albright. You know him?"

After a few suspicious glances passed between the locals, Clint spotted one of them going for his gun. . . . Clint squeezed off one shot in that direction, making sure to clip the man's side without doing any real damage.

Adjusting his aim to the next armed figure, Clint sent another round over the second man's head as that one struggled to close the breech of his rifle after hastily slapping in a few fresh bullets.

A quick scan of the area told Clint that there were no more than the three he'd seen a few minutes ago. He put on an expression of grim ferocity and aimed the Colt at the last man who'd been firing at him. . . . The third man started babbling incoherently.

"Throw that pistol down," Clint barked.

Clint walked up to the other two and kicked their weapons out of reach. "Now we can talk like civilized people," he said while stepping back.

"What the hell do you want here?" The one doing the talking was the oldest of the group and had been the one holding the rifle.

Clint let out a single, humorless laugh. "I sure don't want to be shot at anymore, just like I'm sure you don't want to die today."

DON'T MISS THESE
ALL-ACTION WESTERN SERIES
FROM THE BERKLEY PUBLISHING GROUP

THE GUNSMITH by J. R. Roberts
Clint Adams was a legend among lawmen, outlaws, and ladies.
They called him . . . the Gunsmith.

LONGARM by Tabor Evans
The popular long-running series about Deputy U.S. Marshal
Long—his life, his loves, his fight for justice.

SLOCUM by Jake Logan
Today's longest-running action Western. John Slocum rides
a deadly trail of hot blood and cold steel.

BUSHWHACKERS by B. J. Lanagan
An action-packed series by the creators of Longarm! The
rousing adventures of the most brutal gang of cutthroats ever
assembled—Quantrill's Raiders.

DIAMONDBACK by Guy Brewer
Dex Yancey is Diamondback, a Southern gentleman turned
con man when his brother cheats him out of the family for-
tune. Ladies love him. Gamblers hate him. But nobody pulls
one over on Dex . . .

WILDGUN by Jack Hanson
The blazing adventures of mountain man Will Barlow—from
the creators of Longarm.

TEXAS TRACKER by Tom Calhoun
Meet J. T. Law: the most relentless, and dangerous, man-
hunter in all Texas. Where sheriffs and posses fail, he's the
best man to bring in the most vicious outlaws—for a price.

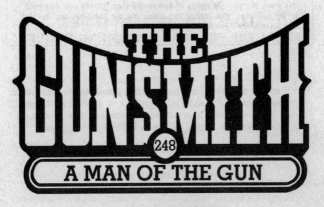

THE GUNSMITH

248

A MAN OF THE GUN

J. R. ROBERTS

J
JOVE BOOKS, NEW YORK

If you purchased this book without a cover, you should be aware that this book is stolen property. It was reported as "unsold and destroyed" to the publisher, and neither the author nor the publisher has received any payment for this "stripped book."

This is a work of fiction. Names, characters, places, and incidents either are the product of the author's imagination or are used fictitiously, and any resemblance to actual persons, living or dead, business establishments, events, or locales is entirely coincidental.

A MAN OF THE GUN

A Jove Book / published by arrangement with
the author

PRINTING HISTORY
Jove edition / August 2002

Copyright © 2002 by Robert J. Randisi

All rights reserved.
This book, or parts thereof, may not be reproduced in any form without permission.
For information address: The Berkley Publishing Group,
a division of Penguin Putnam Inc.,
375 Hudson Street, New York, New York 10014.

Visit our website at
www.penguinputnam.com

ISBN: 0-515-13352-3

A JOVE BOOK®
Jove Books are published by The Berkley Publishing Group,
a division of Penguin Putnam Inc.,
375 Hudson Street, New York, New York 10014.
JOVE and the "J" design
are trademarks belonging to Penguin Putnam Inc.

PRINTED IN THE UNITED STATES OF AMERICA

10 9 8 7 6 5 4 3 2 1

ONE

Most people didn't have to do much to stay out of trouble. In fact, the average man's lifetime was filled with a common string of occurrences that hardly ever got too far away from what most would consider normal. There were good times and bad times, hard times and easy, which would all come together to form an average existence.

Unfortunately, Clint Adams was a far cry from being considered "average."

Unlike the average citizen, Clint spent most of his days on the trail going from one town to another. And when he did manage to settle in a place for more than a day or two, he was given a welcome that was more than just warm . . . it was downright hot.

This was one of those times. And the heat of his reception could be measured only by the blazing lead that filled the air around the small outhouse he'd been forced to use for cover. Clouds of dry dust drifted over the ground after being kicked up by several scurrying feet as they made their way from one spot to another. Small explosions crackled through the air, followed by the distinctive hiss of bullets whipping back and forth.

Clint tried to take a peek around the small closet-sized

structure and was forced to pull his head back immediately as another pair of bullets slapped into the wood next to his face. He didn't look for trouble any more than most other men. The only difference was that trouble had a nasty habit of looking for him.

Drawing in a quick breath, Clint gritted his teeth and thought back to what had started this little mess. It hadn't been anything too fancy or dramatic. All he'd done was ask for directions. The three men resting on the porch of the nearby house seemed friendly enough when they'd asked, "You lookin' to visit someone?"

"I sure am," Clint had replied. "Sean Albright. You know him?"

After a few suspicious glances passed between the locals, Clint spotted one of them going for his gun. The other two followed suit, and rather than shoot down three men, Clint decided to head for cover and try to find out what had ruffled the men's feathers so very badly.

Looking back on it, Clint thought that might not have been a very good decision. After all, the three seemed intent on killing him and the outhouse had been about to collapse under its own weight even before bullets started taking bites out of its sides.

Clint held on to his modified Colt and tensed himself in preparation to break from cover. He had yet to fire a shot. So far, he'd been more than happy to sit back and let the local men pump every one of their rounds into the outhouse. Now, as Clint listened, the gunfire started tapering off and the bursts were being replaced by the clatter of spent cartridges hitting the ground, followed by the occasional curse.

Not wanting to give the men enough time to prepare for another offensive, Clint took advantage of the next lull in gunfire and stepped out from behind the small shack to deliver some fire of his own. The first thing he saw was one of the men taking aim. Clint squeezed off one shot in that direction, making sure to clip the man's side without doing any real damage.

Staggering back with eyes open wide, the man dropped his pistol before pulling its trigger, tripping over his own feet in the process. There was a trickle of blood on his shoulder, which came from a wound that was less serious than a dog bite.

Adjusting his aim to the next armed figure, Clint sent another round over the second man's head as that one struggled to close the breech of his rifle after hastily slapping in a few fresh bullets. Clint's bullet caused that man to dive straight down while covering his head with both hands.

A quick scan of the area told Clint that there were no more than the three he'd seen a few minutes ago. He put on an expression of grim ferocity and aimed the Colt at the last man who'd been firing at him.

The moment he saw that he was in Clint's sights, the third man started babbling incoherently. The gun in his hand began to tremble like the last dead leaf at the end of a branch in the wind.

"Throw that pistol down," Clint barked.

The man didn't even try to keep up a threatening appearance and flung his weapon aside as though the handle had been laying in a fire.

Clint walked up to the other two and kicked their weapons out of reach. Only then did he relax his posture and drop his Colt back into the holster at his side. "Now we can talk like civilized people," he said while stepping back.

"What the hell do you want here?" The one doing the talking was the oldest of the group and had been the one holding the rifle.

Clint let out a single, humorless laugh. "I sure don't want to be shot at anymore, just like I'm sure you don't want to die today. In case you already forgot, all I wanted was a bit of information when you fellas started getting out of hand. Is that the way you always treat newcomers?"

The older man spat on the ground and hitched up his pants. "It is when them newcomers ask about the likes of Sean Albright."

"Yeah," the man with the scratch on his shoulder chimed in. "He ain't welcome around here no more. And the same goes for anyone who calls him a friend."

Clint studied the faces in front of him. After all his years on the trail, he'd come across plenty of different types. If nothing else, his experiences made him a fairly good judge of character. He knew these weren't men with violent natures. If anything, they were simply angry as hell.

And scared.

No amount of posturing could hide the fear that coursed through their souls like a cold river running beneath their skin.

"What has Sean done to warrant all of this?" Clint asked. "Last time I checked, he was a good enough man."

The older man seemed to be pulling himself together a little faster than his companions. He straightened himself up, but knew better than to make even the slightest move toward his weapon. "Then you must not have checked in with him lately. Sean Albright ain't nothing but a coward and a son of a bitch. Wherever he is, I hope he stays there."

"You mean he doesn't live around here anymore?"

"Hell no. We chased him out of town for what he done. There may still be folks around here looking for him. And if they get their hands on him, I can tell you exactly where you can find him."

Holding his shoulder as though he'd been truly hurt, the first local stepped forward with a scowl. "You'll find him in the ground, mister. And if you don't get off my property, I'll see to it that you get a spot right next to that bastard friend of yours, right quick."

The threat barely registered in Clint's mind. He could see through the words, which were so much smoke coming out of the local's mouth. The intent behind them, however, was real enough. Although Clint didn't worry too much about getting harmed by any of these men, he was deeply concerned with what could possibly make them direct so much hate in Sean Albright's direction.

Clint knew he wasn't going to get much more out of the three men. Despite the fact that they'd shot at him, none of the locals seemed interested in fighting any longer. Keeping them all in his line of sight, Clint walked back to where Eclipse was waiting and climbed onto the Darley Arabian's saddle.

"You leavin' town, mister?" the older man asked.

Clint's mind raced with so many questions that his brain seemed to spin inside his head. "I don't have a problem with you men, but you're not chasing me off. If I see you in town, I'll forget about what happened here. But if you don't do the same, I'll remember *real* quickly."

With that, Clint snapped his reins and steered Eclipse back toward the town at the end of the narrow, rutted trail.

TWO

As Clint rode, he barely wasted a thought on the men he left behind. Only a few minutes had passed since those same men had tried to fill him full of holes, but Clint knew those three were just as happy to simply be rid of their target as he was to not be a target any longer. They weren't killers. They were simple people with a huge chip on their shoulders.

And that was what puzzled Clint the most. Why would someone be so angry at and scared of Sean Albright? What could have happened to provoke such a reaction?

Granted, it had been some time since Clint had met up with Albright, but Sean had always been one of the kindest and most generous men he'd ever known. Having served as a scout for the U.S. Cavalry, Albright had proven himself countless times under fire. He was known for leading excursions into hostile territory and even going back into that territory to rescue any men that were wounded or left behind. He would even go back alone, if necessary. Sean had the wounds and medals to prove it.

Clint had met him for the first time over ten years ago. There had been some trouble with Indians raiding coaches and travelers on a pass through the heart of Nebraska. Several mail couriers and folks headed west for California had been robbed and killed by what seemed to be overly protective natives.

Since he was in the area during one of those attacks, Clint had lent his services to help bring those killers to justice. Of all the men who made up the posse, there were only two who weren't out solely for blood. Clint was one of them and Sean Albright was the other.

The crimes had been horrible and some downright gruesome, but the evidence seemed to be too obvious. Each body was laying next to a broken arrow and every carriage had been marked with tribal symbols. That, alone, had been enough to get the posse fired up and screaming for Indian scalps. Since the crimes had hit so close to home, not many of them were willing to look much farther than what they'd been shown.

All they wanted was a target to shoot at and destroy. The simple fact that they could kill in the name of their justice was enough for the men, many of whom had lost friends or relatives in the attacks.

But even then, Clint had been leery of answers that came too easily. The evidence was too neat and there was simply too much of it. Indians could be just as cruel as white men, but they weren't stupid and they didn't have much of a reason to call down the fury of an armed posse when they had enough troubles of their own concerning aggression from settlers and the Army.

At the very least, Clint wanted to be cautious. Maybe even take some time and check into things a little more before hunting anyone down. Nobody in the group seemed to share his view. Nobody, that is, except for Sean Albright.

Sean had been only a few years' removed from his service with the Cavalry and was one of the leaders of the posse. A man roughly Clint's height, he carried at least fifty more pounds of muscle on his burly frame and still somehow managed to move with lightning speed when his life or other lives were on the line. Sean's eyes were steely gray and his hair was black as coal, giving him an intimidating appearance which he used to his advantage whenever he could avoid drawing the customized .45 on his hip.

The posse had been ready to ignore Clint's requests and go off without him. All of those men had been ready to ride out and kill the first man they saw with red skin. All of them, except Sean.

Sean had given Clint a quick, knowing glance before turning to the posse and laying it on the line.

"You men aren't going anywhere," he'd said. "If it's blood you want, then you'll have to take mine." His hand drifted to the gun at his side and his eyes became even colder than steel. "But I'm not about to let you have it without a fight. And I'm not gonna let you slaughter any more innocents just to make you feel better about them that was killed."

The posse started to get riled up, but they weren't about to take on Sean. One of the men stepped forward, the pain and rage inside of his soul burning through to lend his eyes a fiery glint. "But we've seen the markings. We seen what killed them. Hell, we seen the bodies of our own kin stretched out like animals, and you don't want justice?"

"That's exactly what I want. But what you want to do ain't justice. It's murder. All I want is a bit more time. Let's make sure what we're doing before we do it. Otherwise, you all might just be part of something that'll haunt you for the rest of your lives. Believe me," Sean said as the memories came flooding through him. "I know what I'm talking about."

The posse weren't too happy about it, but they stood down. Clint had been ready to back Sean's play, but that hadn't been necessary. They looked into Sean's eyes and saw that the man wasn't about to back down, even if it meant taking a bullet for what he believed. Clint knew from personal experience that guts and convictions rarely traveled hand in hand. When they did, it made for an impressive sight, indeed. Even the enraged posse members had to admire that quality in a man.

Before any of the more bloodthirsty members of the group could get too many ideas in their heads, Sean had stared them all down and given them tasks to perform. Every one of those men wanted nothing more than to extract their vengeance as soon as humanly possible . . . even if they had to go through Sean to do it. And though Sean had seen it just as well, he stood his ground and talked to them like the rational men they weren't.

It didn't take long for all the rest of the posse to be dispatched, leaving Clint and Sean standing in front of the weather-beaten shack that passed for a sheriff's office.

"You did a good job," Clint said. "But you must know they won't hold off for long. They'll go on their hunting party as soon as they think they can get away with it."

Sean nodded. His features hardened even further into a mask of grim determination. "I know. That's why we've got to find who really killed those people before another batch get killed by those sorry wretches."

"You think those wretches might be Indians?"

"Actually, the wretches I was talking about were the ones in that posse of mine."

Both men paused for a second and had a laugh at the comment. Mainly, the moment served to calm the tension that had been building up over the past several minutes. Also, it showed that both Clint and Sean were able to see through the heat of the moment and look for what was really going on.

"So what's the plan?" Clint asked.

Shrugging, Sean walked over to his horse and saddled

up. "Who said I had a plan? I was kinda hoping you might have something up your sleeve."

Even back then, Clint had prided himself on being able to read men just as well as he could read a hand of poker. His skill had become good enough to save his life on several occasions, which meant that he was very rarely surprised.

Despite all his skills, Clint truly hadn't seen that last part coming. "You don't have a plan?" he asked incredulously.

"Nope, but I do think we should check out the Ponca village since they're the closest Indians to these parts. How about we think of a plan on the way?"

Clint shook his head and followed Sean's lead. He knew this man was either very crafty, or very very stupid. Either way, Sean Albright had guts to spare.

THREE

The Ponca Indians lived in a settlement less than ten miles northwest of Briar, Nebraska. Back then Duke, Clint's old horse, had been in his prime. The big, black gelding thundered across the prairie next to Sean's spotted dun to cover the miles as though they were merely there to stretch the animals' legs.

Riding beside the other man, Clint had sensed something about Sean that made him see why others were so quick to follow him. Sean's strength gave his every move an air of confident purpose which made him seem as though he still carried a military rank. Even with his uniform packed away in a chest, Sean had the bearing of someone that should be saluted. His words still rang with true authority.

The Poncas received the two visitors well enough, despite the fact that they'd been the targets of so much hostility from nearly every white man that had been passing through. They were friendly enough to offer Clint and Sean food and water, but they were cautious enough to have someone armed and watching them at all times.

Once the formalities were over with, one of the Indians separated from the rest. He was a man who looked to be in his early to mid-fifties. But, with the hearty constitutions of the natives, he could just as easily have been twenty years older. His skin was darkened by the sun and creased with trenches that had been dug through the years, giving his flesh the appearance of weathered bark. He wore simple clothes with few ornaments besides the beads and symbols that marked him as a member of his tribe.

"What is it you want?" the old man asked in a quietly commanding voice.

Sean stepped forward, motioning for Clint to stay behind. "You know about what's been going on around here lately?"

Nodding, the old man replied, "The murders. Of course."

"How much do you know?"

"We've heard about the deaths and have seen them ourselves. The daughters of one of my people were traveling on one of the coaches that were attacked. It was terrible."

Sean made no effort to hide the surprise on his face. "How old were they?"

"They'd lived less than eight years. Their mother was with them as well. Every one of us still feels the hole they left behind, although their spirits are surely more content after joining with the rest of creation."

Clint hadn't been in Briar for very long, but he'd been there long enough to hear about all of the attacks more than once. And though every story about the attacks had been full of gruesome details, not once had he heard about a group of Ponca children and their mother being counted among the victims.

That little bit of news was monumental. Almost as monumental as the fact that it had been hidden from the public eye.

As they rode away from the Indian settlement, Clint and Sean took a few moments to digest what they'd learned. Finally, once they were certain that they were alone, both men drew their horses to a stop and turned to face each other.

"Do you think that old man was telling the truth?" Sean asked.

Clint only had to think back to the conversation for a minute before nodding. "I don't see why he would lie. Besides, a story like that leaves its mark on a person, and that's an awful hard thing to fake."

"Exactly what I was thinking. Besides, I don't know why he would want to make up something like that."

"Have there been any reprisals from the Poncas?"

"Not as far as I know. Except for the sheriff, I think I'd be one of the first men told if there was."

Clint measured his next words closely. Although he'd quickly grown to respect Sean Albright, he still didn't know exactly how far he could predict what the man would do or where his loyalties truly lay. He could guess all he wanted based on his impression of the man, but even that could be wrong every once in a while.

So when he spoke, Clint made sure to do so very carefully. "There aren't a whole lot of people who could keep information like that under their hats. And if someone wanted to do something like that, it means—"

"It means that he's either the one doing the killing or he's trying to protect the killer," Sean said quickly. "You don't have to spell that out for me. And don't worry none. If this killer turns out to be someone I know, he won't get any pity from me."

"He's got to be one of the men that found the bodies. Maybe even one of the sheriff's deputies."

Sean nodded gravely. "True enough. And he'd have to know enough about the Poncas to know how to set them up. But that last part wouldn't be too hard," he added with a touch of shame crossing his face. "Folks around here would go after the Indians twice as quick as anyone else so long as they had half a good reason."

"I've dealt with my share of Indians," Clint said. "But not the Poncas, specifically. I'm pretty sure they wouldn't slaughter their own people like that."

"Nobody should slaughter other humans like that," Sean growled. "Unfortunately, I know just the type that would be up for it. In fact, I think I know them a little too well for my liking."

They rode the rest of the way in silence. The beating of the horses' hooves against the hard-packed soil thundered in Clint's ears like an explosive storm. All the while, he thought about the attacks and what facts he actually knew about them.

He'd seen the most recent one for himself. At least, he'd seen what was left behind. A small caravan of four covered wagons had been turned over and burned after being stripped down and gutted by the ones who'd killed the people riding inside. Those people had been gutted as well, their bodies left to rot in the dirt like so much trash.

The women's clothes were torn away from their bodies and their throats had been cut. The men lay slumped in their seats, some of them crumpled on the ground after being pitched from their horses. Only one of them had even gotten a chance to draw his gun.

Only one.

Suddenly, Clint felt as though he was remembering the scene through someone else's eyes. And those eyes were much, much clearer.

FOUR

"I'll be damned," Sean said with a slow shake of his head. Squinting his eyes in concentration, he went through his own memories of what had happened, while taking into account what he'd just been told. "You're right, Clint. Only one of those men had his gun out of his holster."

Clint was in the process of figuring every angle he could think of, his eyes darting between Sean Albright and the town of Briar, which was still a few miles in the distance. "I only saw that one, but did you go to the spots where the other attacks happened?"

"Most of them, yeah. Now that you mention it, most of those men were found pretty much the same way."

"Like they were taken by surprise."

Sean shook his head as cold realization swept through him. "It's awful hard to get surprised in the middle of the prairie. Especially by a bunch of wild Injuns."

This was where Clint thought he might have to tread even more carefully. "And if anyone could get close enough to those people without raising any suspicions," he said. "It would be the law . . . or a posse."

Although the words seemed to definitely strike a nerve with Sean, none of the anger he felt was directed toward

Clint. Instead, he stared ahead intently, scowling at the town of Briar as though he could already see the face of the murderer. "You know something? With this in mind, I don't think we'll have to look too far to find the one who's behind all of this. All we have to do is find the man who knows the Poncas well enough to set them up. Someone who is so cold that he'd even hide the bodies of women and children after watching them die."

"Do you know someone like that?"

"I wish to hell I didn't, friend."

When they'd ridden back into town, Clint looked at the faces of the posse members with a new perspective. At least one of those men was a cold-blooded killer. And quite possibly, some of the town's law had just as much blood on their hands, if not more.

It was plain to see that Sean was a changed man as well. His normally friendly manner had become colder and more distant. The man's eyes bore a resemblance to the surface of a frozen lake in the dead of winter. And when the members of the town's posse gathered around him, Sean dropped down from his horse and planted his feet, ready for anything that might happen in the next couple of seconds.

"We did just what you said," one of the posse's spokesmen reported. "There won't be a stage that leaves town without at least two guards."

"And what about the people spreading all those stories about the attacks?" Sean asked.

"We talked to them, as well. I don't think they know anything else but what they been saying. It all still sounds the same. Them damn Injuns did this to put some money in their pockets. We all know they don't mind killin' so long as they get something out of it."

Turning to look at the spokesman head-on, Sean locked eyes with the man and kept them there for a tense couple of seconds. "Oh really? Do we all know that?"

The spokesman was a tall farmer with a stocky build. His dusty blond hair was cut close to the scalp and his hands were covered with calluses earned throughout years of hard labor. "Well . . . yeah," he said with conviction. "I was there. I seen them bodies for myself."

"I know you did, Mike. In fact, you were the one who found the first bodies. Isn't that right?"

Mike nodded once, his brow furrowed. "Damn right. I seen them with my own eyes, just like I seen every one after that."

Sean nodded also, except his movement was slower and more contemplative than the sharp shake of the head given by the farmer. "You volunteered for that duty. To help the sheriff."

Becoming visibly disturbed by the way the conversation was going, Mike took a step back and looked quickly at the men on either side. He then looked back up at Sean and Clint, the suspicion in his eyes becoming tainted by the slightest hint of aggression. "Sheriff Daltry's too old to go riding out of town, especially when there might be shooting."

"And his deputies," Sean said. "What about them? There was no reason to bother them until you knew for sure what had happened, right?"

"I told you all this before," Mike said. "What's this all about? Why are you asking all these questions? What did them Injuns tell you? Whatever it was, you know it was a damn lie! Or was it him?" he asked, jabbing a finger at Clint. "He's been riding around here like he owns the place even though he's only been here for what . . . a week or two?"

Mike's hand fell to rest upon the handle of his gun. Clint spotted the gesture as soon as it had started, but held off on doing anything about it since he was certain that Sean had seen it, as well. Making sure to keep his move-

ments slow and easy, Clint dropped down from the saddle
and stood just behind and to Sean's right.

"Never mind what the Indians told me," Sean said.
"Don't even worry about what anyone's been saying. All
I want to talk about is what you've been saying . . . or
rather, what you *haven't* been saying."

Mike did his best to calm himself down. He let out a
troubled breath and tried to disguise it as a laugh. He took
another step back and tried to pass it off as a simple shift
of his feet. "I told you everything I saw, Sean. Hell, I was
even quoted in the newspaper."

"I know. I read it. So how come you never told anyone
about the children?"

Clint knew that Sean would be building up to this.
Everything he'd said and everything he'd done had been
leading to this particular moment. And the way Mike reacted to those words would show just how much blood
was truly on his hands.

FIVE

For a second, Mike looked just as shocked and surprised as any innocent man would look. But then, that expression cracked around the edges. Like a mirage that had been dropped for the briefest of instants, the man's expression flickered away just long enough to give Clint and Sean a glimpse at what truly lay beneath it.

"Children?" Mike asked. "I . . . I don't—"

"Oh, I'm sure you do," Sean interrupted. "I'll bet that if you think real hard, you'll remember exactly what I'm talking about. In fact, you probably don't have to think very hard about it at all. Those faces are probably burned into your skull like a nightmare, aren't they? Staring back at you every night, their eyes wide with fear."

Clint watched the other men in the posse as the conversation progressed. Their faces reflected true confusion mixed with disgust at the images Sean was dredging up. They looked shocked and appalled at the accusations flying back and forth. Unfortunately, they were much more convincing than Mike, himself.

Some of the other men looked to Mike or Sean, unsure of who or what to believe. A few of them voiced their questions or concerns, but none of them got through to either of the two men, who were only listening to each other. Mike heard nothing but the images being described by Sean. And Sean saw nothing but the guilt which spread across Mike's face like a fungus.

"You know exactly what I'm talking about," Sean stated. "I can see it in your eyes. I've been a soldier in combat more bloody years than you could know and I can spot the ghosts that come with killing. Them ghosts stick with you, don't they? And the screaming . . . it just doesn't stop."

Mike didn't say another word. He didn't have to. All he could do was stare at Sean's face, knowing that no lie he could come up with would be enough to cover up what he'd done. It was as though his soul had been laid bare for all to see.

Just to square away any doubt he might have had, Sean asked, "Why would you do it? Why kill so many people? Just for the money? Or did you get a taste for it? Did the gun just feel too good in your hand?"

"It wasn't nothing like that," Mike replied, his voice now starting to tremble. "If I didn't get some money, I'd lose everything. And if I lost everything, I'd be nobody."

"So you killed all those—"

"I only killed who I had to," Mike cut in, sealing his own fate. When he spoke this time, his voice seemed to be coming from someplace far away. Someplace buried deep inside of him. He looked up as though he stared up from the bottom of a well, his eyes glazing over and his lips quivering like those of a scared child. "Them Injuns never leave nobody alive. I heard that plenty of times. I . . . had to kill all of them if . . . if anyone would believe me."

"But the Injuns don't kill their own," Sean added. "Even you figured that they wouldn't be so coldhearted that they would kill their own people."

Sean didn't have to say anything else for his point to be made. And upon hearing the words, Mike understood what was being said. His eyes locked back at Sean as something inside of him snapped. Suddenly, he was no longer the same man that Clint had known for the short time he'd been in Briar. That man was gone now, replaced by the animal that Sean had been talking about the entire time.

Sensing this, Sean reached out with both of his hands and took a cautious step forward. "This doesn't have to end here and now. You can have your day in court and face up to what you've done. You can take your punishment like a man."

Mike convulsed like a man possessed and pulled away from Sean. As he wheeled around, he pushed away the other members of the posse, who barely seemed to comprehend what was happening.

Clint could sense the tension crackling in the air. He watched as Mike's hand drifted onto the handle of his gun and then away. Back and forth and back again, mirroring the conflicting thoughts that must have been running through his mind. Although Clint didn't know the man well enough to say if he wanted to kill the rest of the posse in an attempt to get away, he did know that Mike was desperate enough to do just about anything. After all, a man capable of murdering women and children didn't have much else to lose in killing a few more.

Without taking another step forward, Sean spoke in a soothing, reassuring manner. "I know you couldn't have done this alone. Whoever you were riding with, there's no reason for them to get away without paying their dues also."

Every one of Mike's muscles tensed. His eyes stopped twitching from face to face and settled exclusively on Sean. Even from where he was standing, Clint could see the cruelty in those eyes. In fact, he wondered at how such a savage personality could hide so well within the farmer's normally passive body.

"No matter what you've done," Sean continued, "you can at least end it by doing the right thing. Tell me who you were working with so we can make sure this doesn't happen again. It's the least you owe to those people that died for the sake of the few dollars in their pockets."

Hearing that, Mike seemed to break just a little bit more. It didn't take a mind reader to figure all the horrors that were racing through the killer's head at that moment. And mixed among all that, there was the constant desperation which rolled off the man like an invisible fog.

Mike looked from side to side, checking to see if the other members of the posse would stick with him or let him face his fate alone. Noticing this, Clint also checked the other men's faces and was surprised to see that all but one of them seemed ready to act at Mike's side.

This only gave Mike the confidence he'd been looking for, and when he turned back to face Sean, he did so with a defiant scowl. "You got nothing on me and you know it."

"Just your own word," Sean replied. "Unless you think I'm going to forget about everything I saw and heard just now."

"You could forget it. Just move along . . . and I'll see that you get a cut of the money we stole in those jobs. Two of them stages were carrying lockboxes, you know. That wasn't no small change in there."

Sean held his ground. The offer didn't so much as put a dent in his resolve. "I don't want a cent of that blood money."

Those words brought all of Mike's desperation to a head, and when he held his hand over his gun, his eyes took on the quality of a starving animal. "That offer goes for you men as well," he said to the rest of the posse. "The jobs are finished. You don't have to do anything besides back my story . . . and help me take out this son of a bitch who would rather put his friends in jail than let them have a comfortable life."

Sean knew it was too late to try talking to them. As much as he'd tried to make it otherwise, the situation had gone beyond all hope of being turned around. Clint knew this just as well, and when he saw that the others were indeed going to take the easiest way out, he moved forward to stand at Sean's side.

"No, Clint," Sean said with a raised hand. "Stay back. This is between me and these here men. I won't have anyone else dragged into it."

Clint was going to protest, but he saw that Sean was also beyond words, and the determination in his request was enough to get Clint to step back and wait to see what was going to happen.

For a moment, Mike and the posse stared straight ahead, waiting for Sean to make a move. The one posse member who'd been undecided seemed to have sided with the killer, if only because it seemed to be the smartest bet.

There was safety in numbers and those numbers were most definitely stacked against Sean Albright. He ignored this fact, however. Even when he was staring down the barrels of four drawn pistols.

SIX

Even ten years ago, Clint had seen more gunfights than he could count. Every one of them had its own personality, like the final act of a small, frenzied play. Some were fought for revenge or anger. Some were drunken mistakes or heated disagreements. Others were simple misunderstandings that had gotten way out of hand. And then there were the ones that were simply inevitable.

This, Clint knew, was one of those.

Sean had tried so hard to keep the lead from flying, but to no avail. Mike was simply not going to deal with his crimes and was convinced that he could get away with them so long as his accuser was dead as well. And now that he had more men to back him up, his convictions were even stronger.

Clint's first reaction was to draw his Colt and do his best to keep Sean alive. But by the time he'd cleared leather, his help was no longer required.

The posse was made up of four men altogether, plus one other who wasn't fast enough to draw before everyone else. One of the most remarkable things that Clint saw was that Sean had the presence of mind to pick that man out and shoot at all the others first.

Mike was the first one to actually move for his gun. The rest of the posse was right behind him, every one of them drawing before Sean had gotten to his pistol. When the first shot rang out, it didn't come from Mike or any of his men. Rather, it was the first thunderous roar issued by Sean's .45.

Clint hadn't even seen Sean draw. One moment, he was standing there waiting calmly and the next, he was blasting Mike clean off his feet. For the first time, Clint finally got an idea of what others saw when they watched his own battles. And even someone as accomplished as Clint Adams couldn't help but be impressed.

Normally, Clint saw things in a gunfight as though they were slowed down. But since he wasn't in this particular fight just yet, his eyes witnessed everything in real time. And if he had blinked just once . . . he would have missed it.

The next shots fired came in quick succession. First, one from Mike's gun as his twitching muscles clamped down on the trigger in the last spasm before death. The next two were other members of the posse firing in sheer panic, their shots either hissing into the air high over Sean's head or digging into the ground at his feet.

Sean's eyes were passive. They took in everything around him without the slightest bit of emotion, which would have only served to slow him down. Rather than let himself become angry or even worried for his own life, Sean simply picked his next target, aimed and fired.

One of the posse's members had collected himself to take more careful aim, but Sean's bullet punched a hole through his skull and dropped him to the ground.

Another of the men who'd decided to stand by Mike's side fired again out of self-preservation, but this time he wasn't even looking at his target. The gun bucked in his hand just as a chunk of hot lead drilled through his chest. Somehow, he still managed to fire a last shot, which whipped through the air less than an inch from Sean's face.

Despite the near-miss, Sean didn't even twitch. Instead, he shifted his aim and squeezed his trigger to put down the last remaining target.

Clint watched all of this without entirely believing it. Even though Mike and his cohorts had been less than ten feet away from Sean, they'd managed to wind up on the losing end of the fight. And though Clint had reflexively drawn his Colt to cover Sean's hide, it seemed his gun wasn't needed this time. All that remained was the one member of the posse who hadn't been able to pull himself together well enough to even draw his gun.

Sean stepped up to that man and stared down at him over the barrel of his .45. "You made a bad decision standing with that killer," he said simply. "You can start making better decisions if you tell what you know to a judge."

Watching this, Clint was ready for the last man to make his move. But once again, he found that Sean had everything under control just fine without him.

"I'll do it," the shaking posse member whimpered after dropping to his knees as though he was praying to his savior. "I'll say whatever you want, just please don't shoot me."

Sean nodded slowly, holstered his gun and offered his hand to the trembling figure at his feet. "All I want is for you to say the truth. How much do you know about what happened?"

"I . . . I heard some things."

"You were with Mike when he went to see the bodies, weren't you?"

"Yes . . . yes I was."

"And did you see the ones I was asking him about?"

Clint knew that Sean was beating around the bush just to make sure that the shaking man wasn't just going to

parrot back everything he was asked in an attempt to save
his skin. Once again, Clint had to admire him. It would
have been just as easy to force him to confess to everything, especially when he had the man completely at his
mercy.

The trembling man nodded. Tears began streaming
down his face, making clean little trails in the dust and
grit that covered his skin. "The children. There were two
of them. They couldn't have been more than six or seven
years old. They were curled up with their momma . . . a
pretty Injun gal with long black hair . . ."

Once the man got started, the words spilled out of him
like rainwater. Most of what he said could have been
learned from Sean's earlier words, but there were plenty
of little things that had only been said by the old man at
the Ponca settlement. It was enough to convince Clint and
Sean that he was telling the truth. The man had, indeed,
seen those horrible things. In fact, that was what had kept
him from jumping to Mike's side when the gunfight
started.

Sean let the man keep talking, even when his words
became nothing more than incoherent rambling. When he
helped the man to his feet, he turned to start leading him
to the sheriff's office.

Clint turned as well, which was the moment when he
saw that they weren't alone on that street.

SEVEN

Both Clint and Sean froze for a second when they saw all those others. In a way, it felt like an invasion of privacy to have so many witnesses to such a climactic moment.

But none of the faces looked upon them with anger. And none of the watchers held guns in their hands or even so much as made a move toward them. Instead, the observers were simple townspeople.

In fact, it appeared as though every single one of Briar's residents had been drawn to the scene, if not by the shouting, then surely by the gunfire.

Clint stood still for a second before realizing that he still held his Colt in hand. After quickly holstering the pistol, he moved to the trembling man's other side so he and Sean could each take one of the man's arms over his shoulder. Once he felt he was being supported, the posse member put his weight on both men, his feet barely touching the ground.

As they walked to the sheriff's office, Sean and Clint looked at all the faces turned in their direction. While some were more shocked than others, there was one thing common among all of them: awe.

Every eye was wide with wonder, and when Clint and

Sean stepped into the sheriff's office to hand over their prisoner, they could hear a few shouts from the crowd outside. Those shouts quickly spread, followed by applause as well as several congratulatory cheers.

"Sounds like you have some admirers," Clint said once the posse member had been dumped into a chair.

"I wouldn't think too much of it," Sean replied. "You should hear them at a hanging."

"Do you think the sheriff was involved in any of those attacks?"

"If you're asking whether or not I can trust him, your guess is as good as mine. All I know is that once he gets here, he'll handle the rest of this mess and I can be done with it once and for all."

Just then, the front door opened and the town's sheriff strode inside. He was a bulky man with the build of someone who'd been happily married to one of the best cooks in Briar for no less than two decades. His wide, fleshy face was beaming with anger or pride, although it was hard to tell which one, since most of his mouth was covered by a thick mustache.

"I thought I'd seen one of everything, boy," the sheriff said. "First you face off with half a dozen men and then you deliver the last one right to my office. How the hell did you do it?"

At first, Sean didn't know quite how to react. "It wasn't that many men. There were only three or four . . ."

Stepping forward, the sheriff looked as though he might try to take a swing at Sean. But instead, he reached out and slapped him heartily on the shoulder. "Hell, I don't care if it was a baker's dozen. All that matters is that someone did something about them vigilantes before they did any more damage to this town. You stood your ground and lived to tell the tale." By this time, a wide smile could be seen beneath his whiskers and his voice boomed

throughout the office. "I only heard what happened sec-
ondhand. Tell me all about it."

Clint watched all of this, wondering if the sheriff even
knew he was in the room. Rather than bust in on Sean's
moment, he made himself useful by making sure the prisoner wasn't about to try slipping out a side door amid the
confusion.

"The attacks on the stagecoaches," Sean began. "They
weren't done by Indians after all."

"Really?" The sheriff had parked himself behind his
desk and was hanging on Sean's every word. "How'd you
come by that information?"

EIGHT

Half an hour later, Sean and Clint were out of the sheriff's office, having left by a back door to avoid the lingering crowd. Both men were even more dazed now than when they'd been in the heat of the gunfight. The voices of the people gathered out front could still be heard from the back alley. Locals shouted out to see Sean's face or shake his hand.

"Sounds like a damn circus," Sean growled.

Clint shook his head. "Better get used to it. You gave them a show they won't soon forget."

"Yeah, yeah. You said that once already." Stopping in his tracks, Sean wheeled around to look back at the sheriff's office. "Did you hear that man in there?"

"You mean the sheriff?"

"He drank up every word I said like it was thirty-year-old Scotch. All he wanted to know was if Mike and the rest were dead or not."

Clint had noticed the same thing. The way the lawman had leaned forward and paid rapt attention to only the bloodiest of details didn't sit well with him at all. In fact, the more Clint had watched the sheriff, the more he'd been convinced of one thing.

"Do you think he was in on those attacks?" Sean asked as though he'd been reading Clint's mind.

"Look," he said while trying to brighten his expression. "One thing I can say for certain is that those attacks aren't going to happen anymore. At least, not from that group of robbers."

"That wasn't my question, Clint. Do you think the sheriff was one of them robbers?"

As much as Clint wanted to just put the day behind him and let Sean do the same, he simply respected the other man too much to lie straight to his face. "If I had to hazard a guess . . . I'd say he was in on it. He just seemed too happy that Mike and his men were dead and not interested enough in what led up to it."

Sean turned on the balls of his feet and slammed his fist into the wall of the building next to him. "Dammit," he hissed under his breath.

"If it makes you feel any better, I still think the attacks are over," Clint said. "As long as that sheriff has half a brain in his head, he'll see that this is the perfect opportunity to get out of his game for good."

"Yeah. He gets to pack up and enjoy his money without paying for all the blood he spilled to get it."

"Look, Sean. I don't like it any more than you do, but we don't have a whole lot to go on besides our gut feelings on this. And we'd need a hell of a lot more than that to start hunting down a lawman without becoming wanted men ourselves. Maybe you should just let this go before you get hurt. I mean, your luck held out pretty damn well today. Don't push it or it just might be the worst mistake you ever make. It could also be your last."

Looking at Clint, Sean gritted his teeth as though he was trying to bite through a bullet. "I haven't known you for very long, Clint. How come you're trying to look after my interests so much?"

"Because you're a good man. And I hate to see bad

things happen to good men. And there's not a lot of good that could happen if you decide to go after a lawman who's already killed women and children."

"I ain't helpless," Sean said, his voice taking on a steely edge.

"No, but you're still human. And after what you did out there today, if that sheriff decides to come after you, he'll do it from an ambush or by surrounding you with twice as many men as you went against."

"Then help me prove what he did, and we can both take him down. You can't tell me that in good conscience you could let someone like that get away. He needs to pay, Clint."

Clint stared into Sean's eyes and took stock of what he saw there. Although he didn't know everything about the man, he knew that his heart was in the right place. More than that, both of their guns combined would be more than enough to take down a crooked small-town sheriff and his deputies.

They'd started walking again, sticking to the alleys and side streets until they were well away from the sheriff's office. By this time, the sounds of voices had died down and the crowd in the street had dispersed. Clint was no stranger to helping people against much worse odds than the ones posed by the sheriff of Briar, Nebraska. What caused him to hesitate before taking on this particular task was Sean, himself.

Although he didn't carry himself as a gunfighter, Sean Albright sure moved like one. But judging by the reaction of the locals, even they hadn't guessed at Sean's prowess after seeing the man for all the years he'd lived among them.

More than anything else, Sean reminded Clint of himself. He saw the other man as though he was standing at the beginning of a road that Clint, himself, had already traveled. The only problem with such a road was that there was no getting off it once the journey began.

"It's not going to stop, you know," Clint said after a few minutes of silence had passed.

"What?"

"Those people. The stories they're going to tell and the tales they'll make up about you will start today and they won't stop."

Sean looked confused for a second and then his face broke into a wide smile. "Oh, that's not anything to worry about. We just don't get a lot of gunfights in Briar. Not like you're used to, anyway."

"You never told me you could handle a gun like that."

"I learned when I was a kid. Always had a knack for it. When I joined the Cavalry I got some more practice. Hell, I ain't even hardly fired it for years."

"Trust me," Clint said. "That fight impressed me and I've seen a hell of a lot of them. I've been *in* a hell of a lot of them, so I'm not impressed too easily. You'd better get used to being a local celebrity around here."

Sean turned to Clint and crossed his arms on his chest. "Is that how you got started?"

Clint had just been thinking about that very thing. "Not exactly, but it's close enough to stir some memories. Once you walk away from something like that and there are enough witnesses around, the rest takes on a life of its own after a while, and before too long, you've got yourself a reputation."

Shrugging, Sean started walking again. "There can't be much harm in that. Let 'em talk if it keeps them busy. I've got bigger things to worry about right now."

"That's what I wanted to tell you. A reputation is a big thing, especially if it's for being handy with a gun. A lot of people out there work their whole lives to get a reputation for themselves and they don't mind taking one from someone else who's already earned it."

That brought Sean to a stop again. "What are you driving at?"

"Just a friendly warning, that's all," Clint said. "And I know what I'm talking about on this subject."

"I'll bet you do, Gunsmith."

Clint nodded. "My point exactly. Since I got that name branded onto my hide, I've had more young gunfighters than I can even count come after me. And you know what they're after? My blood. Just because it came from The Gunsmith, they want my blood so they can brag about it to their friends and anyone else who'll listen, hoping that someday other people will start talking so they can get that reputation they've been wanting so much."

"But I'm not you, Clint. I'm nowhere close."

"Not yet, but it's started. Whether you wanted it or not, it's started. Now's the place where you can avoid getting branded like me. Just lay low and stay out of trouble. Don't give them anything else to tell stories about and the tales will stop. Flash that gun around any more and you'll be on your way to your own little legend."

All Sean could do was keep shaking his head. "I can think of worse things to be than a living legend."

"So can I. You might wind up a dead one."

NINE

Thinking back to those times all those years ago, Clint was hardly aware that he'd arrived in the town of Lumley, Kansas. The house where he'd asked directions seemed to be another lifetime away, and though his body was in the present time, his mind was still back in Briar where he'd first met Sean Albright.

Clint shook his head in wonder that all of that had happened only ten years ago. That was a pretty good chunk of time by any stretch of the imagination, but it seemed so much longer the more he thought about it. Mainly because so much had happened in those ten years. So much had changed that Clint and Sean were barely the same people any longer.

At that moment, Clint remembered what the local men had said about Sean when he'd first arrived on the outskirts of town. They'd called him a cowardly son of a bitch and cursed his name with every breath they could pull into their lungs.

In all the time that had passed since that first impressive gunfight a decade ago, Clint had heard plenty of things about Sean Albright. Some had been a bit on the exag-

gerated side and others had been outright lies. But never
had he heard Sean called names like those.

Even if people might have thought the labels fitting,
they wouldn't have had the guts to say them out loud.
Clint flicked Eclipse's reins to hurry the Darley Arabian
down the street to where he thought he'd spotted a livery.
The longer he thought about everything he'd seen and
heard since his arrival, the more Clint wanted to meet up
with Sean and shed some light on the situation.

Lumley was a fairly good-sized town situated a few
miles outside of Fort Scott. It seemed to cater to the sol-
diers who passed through on their way across the border,
and was filled with more than its fair share of saloons and
cathouses. But the place somehow managed to keep from
getting overrun by the element that normally frequented
such establishments, giving Lumley a quiet feel which
was maintained by the constant presence of armed men
in uniform.

It wasn't until he'd dropped Eclipse off in a comfortable stable and was walking down the town's main boardwalk that Clint realized he didn't know exactly where to
find Sean. Last he'd heard from the man, Sean had sent
a letter to Rick Hartman's saloon in Labyrinth, Texas,
inviting Clint to come for a visit whenever he was in the
area.

Granted, that had been over two years ago, but Clint
knew the invitation would be open for as long as it took
for him to drag his carcass back through Kansas. And now
that he was there, Clint had to stop and fish the letter from
his shirt pocket so he could study it quickly for directions.

There were vague instructions leading to a house on the
outskirts of town in the opposite direction from which
Clint had entered. Since he didn't feel like hopping back
onto Eclipse and riding out again on an empty stomach,
Clint looked for the first place he could find that might
serve some food and headed that way instead.

The first place to catch Clint's eye was a steak house on the corner which gave off a smell that nearly brought drool to the corners of his mouth. The scents of cooking meat and freshly baked bread poured from the door which was being opened and closed by a steady stream of hungry customers going in and stuffed ones coming out. Joining the former group, Clint dodged a speeding stagecoach and crossed the street.

Despite the line of people entering the restaurant, Clint was able to get in and get himself a table relatively quickly. Whenever he spotted a plate of hot steaks being brought out from the kitchen, however, the wait seemed to take forever.

But in the space of a few minutes, he was seated and taking the first sips of a cold beer which had been set in front of him by a stout young woman with long blond hair tied up in a bun at the back of her head. She watched Clint take the edge off his thirst before giving him a quick smile.

"What can I get for you?" she asked.

"I'll take one of those steaks I've been smelling and a baked potato. If there's any bread left I'll have some of that as well."

"We've got all that and some stew that just came out of the pot. Care for a bit of that as well?"

"Sounds perfect," Clint said while rubbing his hands together. "The quicker the better."

The waitress gave him a wink and pat him on the shoulder. "For you, handsome, I'll make sure someone else has to wait a bit longer."

"I'd protest, but I'm too hungry. Thanks a lot."

Nodding, she let her hand linger on his shoulder for just a few more seconds before heading back toward the kitchen. True to her word, the blonde returned quick enough to make the tables around Clint eye her suspiciously. She ignored the peeved expressions and set down a plate of piping hot food in front of Clint.

"I think I just found my favorite place to eat in this town," he said while taking up his silverware and carving a piece from the steak. The food melted in his mouth and tasted so good that Clint almost forgot the other reason he'd ridden into Lumley to begin with.

"Enjoy your meal," the waitress said. "Let me know if you need anything else. If you're new in town, I can tell you where all the good hotels are . . . or if there's anything else you might need . . ."

"Actually, there is," Clint said after swallowing the steak in his mouth. "Does Sean Albright still live around here?"

The waitress didn't say a word. She didn't have to. Everything Clint needed to know about what she was thinking or might have felt about what he'd asked her was written all over her face. It was reflected in the sudden coldness in her eyes as well as the severe turn of her mouth into something just short of a scowl.

"I'm an old friend of his and I was just—"

But the waitress had already turned sharply on her heels and walked away. Clint looked around to the nearby tables and discovered that many of the other diners regarded him with similar looks of anger mixed with disgust.

Now, more than ever, Clint wanted to find Sean and get to the bottom of what the hell was going on.

TEN

The room was completely dark, except for the faint trickle of light that managed to sneak through the curtains drawn across a single window. Just one amid a row of such rooms on the second floor of Lumley's biggest cathouse, it was only big enough to hold a bed, dresser and a single chair. Heat from the two bodies inside had managed to fill the air in less than five minutes. A woman's throaty moans mingled with the heat like a mist that covered the skin of the couple entwined on the bed.

Her name was Lara. The man on top of her didn't know her last name, which was nothing out of the ordinary since she never gave her last name to any of her customers. And in the hour they'd known each other, Sean Albright never asked for it.

Lara's slender, sweaty body writhed on the bed beneath him. Tightly muscled legs wrapped around his waist, her ankles locking behind Sean's back. As he pumped into her, Lara's stomach tensed with the effort of pushing her hips up to meet him while her back arched against the mattress.

"Ohh, god," she cried out while raking her nails over his shoulders. "God, yes!"

Sean slid one hand down over her side, his thumb grazing the side of one firm breast. His other hand slipped through the tangle of her strawberry blond hair, pulling it just enough to bring a smile to her face. Every time she moaned, Sean could feel her muscles tense just a little more. Her body clenched around his thick cock, holding onto him tightly as though she didn't want to let him go.

He pulled out of her and let his shaft rub between her legs, giving them both a moment to catch their breath.

"Don't stop," Lara urged, her hand drifting down to grab hold and stroke his penis up and down. "Keep it up or I'll have to go on without you."

Sean smiled and slapped her lightly on her rump. "I'm not through yet, darlin'. Just giving you a chance to breathe."

"I don't want to breathe. I want you to keep fucking me." With that, she got to her knees, turned around and pressed her chest against a pillow. Her back to him, she lifted her hips and arched her back invitingly. Lara's smooth, firm backside wriggled back and forth as she pushed her body toward him.

Sean didn't even try to hold off any longer. Even in the dim light of the room, he could still see the perfect curve of her back as it sloped down to her neck. Lara's ass was perfect and she knew just how to move it so that he wanted nothing more than to feel it in his hands.

Taking her hips in both hands, Sean pushed himself forward until his cock was sliding between her legs. It only took a few simple movements for him to slip into her waiting pussy and then he was once again driving all the way into her creamy depths.

Lara let out another moan, but this time it was much louder. Tossing her head back, she whipped her hair back and forth, her hands making fists around clumps of the bed linen while the man behind her slammed into her again and again.

The sound of her cries soon mixed with that of their bodies slapping together. Sean, too, was groaning now with the building pleasure he felt as he pounded inside Lara's body with reckless abandon. Rivulets of sweat formed at the base of her spine, glistening in what little light there was until it trickled down.

Sean leaned forward so he could move his palms over Lara's skin, massaging her firm buttocks and then working all the way up to her shoulders. Once there, he slipped his hands around and cupped her breasts, gently pinching her hard nipples between thumb and forefinger.

"That's it," she whispered while looking over her shoulder at him. "Just like that."

Once their eyes met, neither one of them wanted to look away. Every time Sean pushed inside of her, Lara's lips would part just a little bit, her eyes narrowing as a jolt of pleasure surged through her body.

Sean slowed his motions now, kneading his hands over the curves of her figure while sliding luxuriously in and out of her. Responding to this, Lara pressed her head against the pillow and shifted her hips while letting out a smooth, satisfied sigh.

Suddenly, Lara's breaths started to quicken. Her sighs turned into a panting rhythm as she clenched her eyes tightly shut. Feeling her muscles contracting around him, Sean took hold of her by the hips and drove his cock deep inside of her.

When their bodies met, Lara cried out louder than she had the entire night. And when he pulled back to pound into her again, Sean saw her head snap up and her hair settle down her back, its ends tickling the slope of her backside.

He knew she was about to climax and his own pleasure was starting to peak as well. When her orgasm came, Lara was unable to make another sound. Every last shred of her voice was pinched off by the waves of ecstasy that swept through her body.

Again and again, her muscles convulsed around his stiff shaft. And the moment they subsided, she pulled away from him and turned around. Without missing a beat, Lara pulled Sean onto the mattress so he could lie down. She straddled his shoulders and lowered her face down between his legs, opening her mouth and allowing his cock to slip between her lips.

She devoured his penis and swirled her tongue around its tip, pressing her lips around the base of his shaft. While moving her hands along the insides of his thighs, she bobbed her head up and down, sucking him loudly.

As much as Sean wanted to continue their lovemaking all night long, he couldn't stanch the tide that was swelling up within him. Her mouth moved expertly over him, and her hands only served to make the sensations that much more intense.

Soon, he could feel the pleasure building up to an explosion. Sean reached down to run his fingers through her hair as she took him all the way in her mouth and ran her tongue up and down the bottom of his penis. That was more than enough to send him over the edge, and he was soon exploding inside of her.

Lara stayed put for a few more seconds, licking him gently as he came down from the heights to which she'd sent him. After lying with him for a minute or two, she was off the bed and standing naked at the dresser, rummaging in the dark for the cotton slip she'd left in a pile along with the rest of her clothes.

Still in the same position she'd left him, Sean rubbed some of the sweat from his eyes and took a deep breath. "Damn, woman. If I didn't know better, I'd say you were possessed."

She laughed without looking back at him. Having found what she'd been looking for, Lara pulled the slip

over her head and turned around after smoothing it down
past her hips.

"I guess I just haven't had it so good in a while," she
said. "Most of the men I see just want to get what they
can get as quickly as they can get it."

"Well, you won't have to worry about them for too
much longer. If I have my way, I'll keep you busy enough
that you'll be able to quit this place and come live with
me."

Her face bore a slightly surprised expression. "Oh really? You're full of surprises tonight, aren't you?"

Sean nodded. It was at that moment that he heard the
footsteps outside his door. He didn't have to hear anything
else before his reflexes kicked in and sent him rolling off
the bed.

"Actually," Lara said as the door came crashing in.
"I've got a surprise or two of my own."

ELEVEN

Sean's reflexes had always been naturally sharp. Ever since he could remember, he'd been able to react when everyone else seemed content enough to just stand by and watch. Those instincts had been further honed during his years of military service and eventually during his own work as a man of the gun.

Those instincts had saved his life more often than any firearm. And it was those same instincts that Sean blamed for bringing his life to its current depths. Even as he dropped onto the floor and reached out to snatch his gun belt from where it hung over the room's single chair, he had enough presence of mind to silently curse himself for daring to think that he'd been able to find a safe spot amid the storm brewing around him.

The first gunshot blended in with the sound of the door crashing against the wall. Sean had his .45 in hand by the time he heard that bullet thump into the mattress he'd only just left behind.

Sean knew better than to hurry into anything blind. All he could see from his current position was a vague outline of Lara's bottom half, and that was only because of the white cotton slip hugging her frame. Watching as she turned and walked calmly toward the door, Sean pushed himself on the floor until his back touched against the wall.

"Took you long enough," Lara said. "I thought you were supposed to be here a few minutes ago."

"What the hell do you care? By the sound of it, you were enjoying yourself enough." Whoever he was, the man didn't sound like he was in any hurry. His voice was calm and collected, if only just a little anxious.

Although Sean didn't recognize the voice, that fact didn't bother him. What concerned him more was that the woman was obviously a part of the double cross. Now he would have to assume she was a threat.

Sean hated fighting women.

It seemed cruel no matter how much they had it coming. But if the last few years of his life had taught him anything, it was that he couldn't afford to get what he wanted if he was going to stay alive.

There were another couple of footsteps from the man, which stopped before he moved around the bed. "Here," he said to Lara. "Take your money and get the hell out of my way."

Sean's lips curled into an angry scowl when he heard the crumple of paper as the bills were snatched from the unknown man's hand.

"I want double," Lara sneered. "You know it's worth it and you can't do this without me."

Sean had heard enough. "I'll give you one chance, dar-lin'," he shouted while making sure to keep his head down. "Clear out of here now and take whatever he gave you. I won't come after you."

"I know that, Sean," she replied. "You won't come after me because you'll be dead in a couple seconds."

Shaking his head, Sean pulled back the hammer of his .45 and tensed himself for the inevitable. He'd known she was going to say something like that. God help him, he'd known but he'd had to give her the chance all the same.

He waited until he heard another footstep. When it came, Sean leapt to his feet and caught the man just as he was about to walk around the bed. One of the stranger's boots was still coming down when Sean's gun barked once in the darkness.

The shot lit up the room in a brilliant spark of light that was gone in a fraction of a second. Even so, he could still see the scene in his mind's eye, which preserved it like a photograph. There was the man's confident expression, which resembled every last one of those that had come before him. And Lara's face was captured as well, her eyes wide and her mouth open in a scream that would be lost amid the thunder.

Sean's bullet caught the stranger in the middle of his chest, the impact lifting him off balance before he could even complete the step he'd been taking. The man's gun was already coming around to point at Sean, but his finger tensed on the trigger prematurely, sending another round into the rumpled bed linens.

His heart beating violently in his chest, Sean aimed and fired again. When he took his shot, he realized something that struck him almost as hard as pieces of lead slamming through his lungs.

He was shaking.

Even as he pulled back the hammer and sent a third round into the stranger's chest, Sean could feel the trembling in his hand and arm. It wasn't enough to pull his aim off center, but it was enough to rattle him all the way down to his soul.

For someone who lived by the steadiness in his hands and the clarity of his mind, even the slightest tremble could spell instant death. In all his years, Sean had only started to feel the shakes a few times. When he was younger, they'd only come when he was drunk. Over the last couple of months, however, they'd been a frequent companion.

Sometimes they came when he drew his pistol, but sometimes they would come for no reason at all. His mind could set them off when he made the mistake of thinking about the constant struggle his life had become. For this moment, the shakes seemed to take hold of him and toss him about like a kicking rabbit inside a dog's mouth. And when he blinked away the sweats that he'd known were soon to come, Sean found himself standing over the stranger's twitching body.

He stood there for a second or two, staring down at the bullet-riddled corpse which had been walking and talking only a few moments ago. What struck Sean the hardest was the man's face. It wasn't a man's at all. Instead, it would have looked more fitting on a boy. Its skin was free of lines and the eyes were still open, staring out hopefully, without even the slightest doubt in his abilities.

Sean remembered when he'd been that full of pride and confidence. He also remembered seeing faces like that before . . . dozens of them . . . maybe hundreds. Every one of those kids had been full of youth and vigor. Every one of them had tracked Sean down like a dog. And every one of them had died with that very same look in his eyes.

TWELVE

Snapping himself out of his contemplations, Sean counted the holes in the young man's body so he could know how many bullets were still in his cylinder. He thumbed back the hammer and twisted around to face Lara, who was still standing near the open door.

She looked like she only wanted to run away as fast as her legs would carry her. But the problem was that her legs couldn't carry her at all. In fact, they barely seemed able to keep the rest of her body upright. "Are . . . are you going to kill me?" she asked.

Sean looked her over. Even with the stranger's money clutched in one hand and a pearl-handled Derringer in the other, she couldn't help but look beautiful. The white cotton slip clung to her body, plastered against her skin by thick layers of perspiration.

Keeping his gun trained on her, Sean reached for the chair and picked up his britches. "So did he pay you to set me up or finish me off?"

Lara glanced at the gun in her hand and quickly tossed it to the floor as if it had suddenly started to burn her. "I was . . . supposed to keep you busy until he . . . got here."

"Then why didn't you run? Why'd you pull that gun

of yours instead of leave when you were supposed to?"

"I don't know," she said meekly. "I wanted to . . . I guess I had to see if . . ."

The shaking in Sean's hand increased until even Lara could see the fits taking hold of him. Only they weren't the same as when they started. By this time, the emotion causing the shakes was stark rage. That fact was plain enough to see in Sean's eyes.

"You wanted to see if you could take me," he said through clenched teeth. "Just like all the others."

Lara searched her mind for something to say. She made her living off of knowing just what words any man wanted to hear and just the right way to let them flow from her mouth, but at the moment when it seemed to count the most, she was unable to come up with a single sentence. Her lips quivered and she forced herself to draw a breath, but the only sound she could make was a shuddering gasp.

The entire time, Sean watched her. Staring over the barrel of his gun, he thought about what he should do with this woman who had done her level best to deliver him into the jaws of death.

"Get the hell out of here," he said finally.

She blinked once, her shoulders dropping from where they'd been bunched up around her ears. "You . . . you're not . . ."

"I wasn't planning on it, but I can sure change my mind."

Taking one slow backwards step, she tested her footing as though she wasn't sure whether or not she could get herself to move. Desperation won out, however, and she took another quicker step out of the room. Her eyes remained locked on Sean's gun. In them, there was a mixture of fear and morbid curiosity.

It could go off at any moment, ending her life in an instant.

Or it could just stare back at her like a dark, unblinking eye.

Sean knew what was going on inside her mind. He'd seen it almost as much as he'd seen the ones who thought they could take him down. She was intrigued by the danger, aroused by walking the line between life and death. Years ago, he'd used that twisted attraction to his benefit. But that was a long time ago. Now . . .

"Go on," he snarled. "I told you to get the hell out of my sight. You're making me sick."

Still a woman, Lara had the nerve to look offended by Sean's comment as she tossed her hair and turned away.

"One more thing, though," he said before she huffed off down the hall. "That money of yours . . . leave it."

Now she looked blatantly pissed. "What?"

Cinching up his pants, Sean managed to keep the .45 aimed in her direction. It wasn't the easiest thing to do, but he'd had a lot of practice. "I said leave that money he gave you."

She threw it into the room, every one of the bills fluttering to the ground like a swarm of dead butterflies.

"And the money I gave you," Sean added with a smirk. "The least I can get out of almost getting killed is a free piece of ass."

Lara's face twisted into a contemptuous scowl. "You're a son of bitch," she spat. "Did you know that?"

"Yeah, I've been told that a lot lately."

Reaching down to a thin garter belt around her left leg, Lara plucked the folded cash she'd taken from Sean before she'd led him up to this room. She held the money up to her mouth, spat on it and pitched it to the floor before storming down the hall.

THIRTEEN

Even if Clint had been blind and deaf, he wouldn't have been able to miss the feeling that he was most definitely no longer wanted inside the restaurant. Any other time, and he might have just paid his bill and left. But his stomach was still running the show, so he polished off the steak and finished his beer before getting up to leave.

There was a certain satisfaction in taking his time in the face of so much overt hostility, but that feeling quickly faded when he saw a few of the patrons flinch reflexively when he merely turned in their direction. They moved as though they thought he might take a shot at them, despite the fact that he hadn't so much as uttered a cross word at any of them.

Rather than try and talk to any of them, Clint simply set his money on the table and walked outside. The instant he cleared the door, he could hear the noise level in the restaurant swell with excited chatter. He couldn't make out any distinct words, but Clint knew well enough what the topic of conversation had to be.

He walked down the street, doing his best to sort through everything flowing through his mind while picking a direction to go. Still a complete stranger to Lumley,

Clint instinctively headed in the direction where he saw the fewest people. Foremost on his mind was to get somewhere he could think.

Before too long, he came across a place that seemed to fit the bill well enough. What really attracted him was the fact that the saloon seemed to be almost completely still. Clint had to walk up to the front window and peek inside just to confirm that the place wasn't in fact abandoned.

But even though there was hardly more than a dull murmur coming from beyond the front door, which stood ajar, and only the faintest flicker of firelight, Clint did manage to pick out a few signs of life. He stepped inside and took a better look around, letting the door swing slowly shut behind him.

The saloon wasn't too big. Most of the room was taken up by the packing crates lined up in a sloppy row to form the semblance of a bar. One man stood with his back against the wall next to an old bookshelf that now held bottles instead of leather-bound pages, and one other stood with all his weight leaning on his elbows. Beyond that, there were only two other souls in the place, and they were engrossed in their own whispered conversation at one of two tables.

Noticing Clint with no small amount of surprise, the man behind the bar stepped up and dusted off a corner of the crates with a tattered rag. "What can I get ya?" he asked.

Clint positioned himself in front of the newly cleaned spot and nodded in greeting. "I'll take a beer if you've got it."

"This is a saloon, ain't it?"

"Sure . . . if you say so."

Rolling his eyes, the barkeep plucked a mug from a stack behind the crates and knelt down until only the top of his head could be seen. "Don't be fooled by looks, mister. This here's the best kept secret in Kansas."

Clint was about to fire back with another jibe, but stopped when his beer was set in front of him. He lifted the glass and swirled the liquid around inside, admiring the clear consistency and tantalizing smell. The liquid rolled down his throat like a wave of clean mountain water, leaving him with a beaming smile.

"Now, that's damn good," Clint said as he set the mug down.

"What'd I tell ya?"

After taking another sip, Clint looked around the deserted place and asked, "With beer like this, how is it you're so empty? No offense, but I've been in places a hell of a lot bigger than this that had swill running through their taps. Aren't there any beer drinkers in this town?"

"Sure," the barkeep said with a troubled groan. "Normally this place is full to the rafters, but whenever . . ."

He trailed off just then as his eyes darted over to the lone man at the end of the bar. Clint looked in that direction also, but saw nothing strikingly different about the solitary figure.

As if he could feel the others' eyes on him, the lone man shifted on his feet and moved his head almost imperceptibly to look at them. "Go ahead and say what you wanted to say, Elden. Normally this place is packed, but nobody wants to share any space with me."

Squinting in the dim lighting to get a better look at the figure, Clint moved down the bar, taking his beer with him.

"Then again," the man said while straightening up, "I've never known Clint to be a very good judge of character."

"Sean? Is that you?" Clint asked as his eyes grew wide. "I've been looking all over for you."

"Yeah . . . you ain't the only one."

FOURTEEN

It took Clint a moment or two before he realized that he was truly looking at the man he'd been searching for. "I can't believe it's really you," he said, trying not to sound as concerned as he felt. "I, uhh . . . almost didn't recognize you."

Sean walked over to Clint and held out his hand. They exchanged a friendly greeting, but when Clint tried to take his arm back, he found that Sean was still hanging on. Even though the motion was slow and easy, Clint nearly pulled Sean off his feet.

"You're drunk," Clint stated.

A wry smile came across Sean's face as he nodded slowly. "Yes, sir. I most certainly am." He wobbled on his feet as though the simple nod of his head was enough to send him straight to the floor. His reflexes were still somewhat with him, however, and his hand shot out to grab hold of the bar and steady himself at the last second.

Clint's first reaction was to reach out and help the other man, but when he tried to take Sean's elbow, he was quickly rebuked.

"I don't need any help," Sean snarled. "Jus' leave me alone." Once he'd regained his balance, he took a deep

breath and stared at the bar in front of him as though he
was seeking guidance from the half-empty bottle he'd left
there. After he'd watched the liquor slosh back and forth
a couple of times, he turned his attention back to Clint.
"What are you doin' here, anyway? I thought you were . . .
somewhere in Colorado or Wyoming or something."

Watching Sean carefully, Clint set his beer down closer
to where the other man had been standing. "I've been in
Texas lately, but you know me. I'm always dragging my
carcass to one end of the country or another."

"Yeah . . . I know you."

Clint took a few slow sips of his beer. Suddenly, the
brew didn't taste as good as he'd remembered. It didn't
take long before he realized the bitter taste in his mouth
had nothing at all to do with what he'd been drinking.
"You celebrating something, Sean?"

The only reply he got was a rasping grunt.

Turning to the bartender, Clint asked, "How long has
he been here?"

The pale, sunken-faced man hesitated for a couple of
seconds. His eyes flashed toward Sean, obviously uncomfortable with saying anything in front of him.

"It's all right," Clint assured him. "I'm a friend. Just
seeing how far I have to go to catch up with him."

"Only about half an hour or so," the barkeep said. "But
in that time you'd have to polish off half of a bottle plus
another one on top of it. That should bring you up to
flush."

The surprise on Clint's face was followed by disbelief.
In the time he'd known Sean, he never knew the man to
drink more than every once in a great while. And even
then, it was barely enough for the average man to feel the
effects of the alcohol in his system. But when he gave the
barkeep a questioning look, he got a solemn nod in response. And when the man selling the whiskey looked

concerned about someone's drinking, that was never a good sign.

Clint leaned against the bar, felt the crates shift beneath him, and then took some of his weight off of them again. "What's the occasion?" he asked.

Sean's breaths were coming in deep, ragged gasps that sounded hard and painful. They reminded Clint of the times he'd spent with men dying of consumption . . . or drinking themselves into an early grave.

"Since when do I need an occasion?" Sean asked. "Can't a man just have a drink after a hard day's work?"

"Sure, but it sounds to me like you've been drinking enough for the last year's worth of hard days. It's not like you."

"What the hell do you know?" Sean snarled as he wheeled around to face Clint head-on. The motion almost took him off his feet, but Sean managed to keep himself upright. "I haven't seen you in . . . what . . . five years? What the hell do you know about what I am . . . or what I've done?"

Now Clint knew he was getting somewhere. "What have you done, Sean? Besides become a sorry drunk, I mean."

A fire shone in Sean's eyes, which was the most life Clint had seen in the other man since the conversation had begun. Unfortunately, that fire was more than a sign of life. It was a sign of rage that Clint was all too familiar with.

Sean let the anger build inside of him until it had nowhere else to go but out. And when he staggered forward again, he led with a vicious right hook aimed directly for Clint's jaw.

Any other time, and Sean might have gotten the punch in. This time, however, he might as well have announced the punch with a telegram hand-delivered by a marching band.

Clint didn't move until he was certain Sean would follow through with the punch. Even so, he managed to square his shoulders and catch the other man's fist before it got within a few inches of landing on its intended target.

"What the hell are you doing, Sean?" Clint asked as his hand closed in tightly around Albright's fist.

"Trying to knock you on your pompous ass!"

The two spent the next two seconds glaring across at each other, each one waiting for the next move to come his way. As the tension started to fade, Clint looked around and noticed that everyone else in the saloon was staring intently at them.

Pulling his fist from Clint's grasp, Sean took a somewhat steadier step toward him and flung out his left hand in a looping motion. This time, however, he aimed for Clint's shoulder and landed with an open-handed slap. "Let's get out of here, friend," Sean said with a laugh. "If I create another scene around here, the folks will expect regular shows."

Although Clint was definitely confused about Sean's behavior, he was more than happy to escort him into the fresh air and away from his bottle. Sliding his arm beneath Sean's elbows and around his back, Clint nearly hefted the man off his feet. "Come on," he said while grunting slightly under the weight. "I've got you."

FIFTEEN

The pair walked for an hour or two. Actually, Clint did most of the walking, while doing his best to support Sean's weight. Before too long, Sean stopped his nonsensical babbling, which had run all the way from violent threats to bawdy jokes. Finally, some of the drunkenness started to wear off and the man Clint knew began to reemerge.

"Awww, Jesus," Sean said. "If you don't stop dragging me around, I'm gonna toss my dinner onto your boots."

Clint set the man down on the edge of the boardwalk next to a horse trough. "Headache starting to kick in, huh? You might want to splash some water on your face to sober you up."

Laughing under his breath, Sean leaned forward and stared at his reflection in the dirty water. "To hell with you, Clint. Jus' leave me alone before I knock you on your ass and stomp—"

The lengthy threat was cut short when Clint grabbed a handful of hair from the back of Sean's head and pushed him face-first into the trough. Clint shook his head and counted to three, keeping Sean in the water no matter how much he struggled. When he pulled him out again, Clint leaned back to avoid the spray of water as Sean shook his head like a dog coming in from the rain.

"You feel any better?" Clint asked.

The only answer he got was a sputtering string of obscenities laced with the occasional unkind reference to Clint's mother. Clint couldn't help but laugh to himself as he pushed Sean back into the water, this time counting an additional five seconds.

Pulling Sean up again, Clint asked, "How about now?"

Sean spit out a stream of water and started hacking for air. He tried to talk, but couldn't get out much more than a few coughs before waving his hands in surrender. His hair was soaking wet and a few dead leaves that had been floating in the trough now stuck to his face.

Finally, Sean cleared his throat enough to get a few words out. "All right . . . all right. You . . . made your . . . point."

Clint started to help Sean away from the trough, but saw that he was already becoming more steady on his feet. When he stepped back, Clint still made sure he was ready to catch the other man if necessary. To Clint's surprise, however, Sean took a few deep breaths and wiped the water from his eyes before stretching his arms high over his head.

"Did you have to go and do all that?" Sean asked while plucking a leaf from his cheek. "Coffee works just as well, you know."

"Sure, but coffee isn't half as much fun."

They looked at each other once again, except this time there was no tension at all. When they laughed, it reminded Clint more of the way he remembered them laughing, and Sean was more like the man he'd met all those years ago in Briar.

"Dammit if it ain't good to see you, Clint. I didn't even know you were coming out this way."

"I didn't know either until it happened. Actually, I had

to make a run out to Oklahoma a while back and eventually found myself in your neck of the woods so I thought I'd drop by. Hope you don't mind."

"Mind?" Sean asked. "Not at all. You might have caught me on a better day than this one, but that doesn't mean I'm not glad to see an old friend like yourself."

Clint studied Sean carefully. He watched the way the other man moved and the way he carried himself. He even listened to the careful way he spoke, forming every syllable like a kid standing at the front of the schoolroom. "I almost didn't recognize you back at that saloon. In fact, I can't recall a time when I've ever seen you even half that drunk before."

"Like I said . . . it's been a rough day."

"You must get a lot of those."

"Why do you say that?"

"Because a man doesn't clear a bottle and a half of whiskey out of his head this fast unless he's had a hell of a lot of practice."

"Jesus, Clint, I never thought I'd see the day when you became a preacher. If you're looking for donations, I'm fresh out."

Clint could tell he wasn't getting anywhere this way, so he decided to take a different route. "You're right. Sorry about that. It's just that I wanted to make sure you were all right. That's all."

"You always did your best to look out for me, didn't you? Even when you knew I could hold my own against anyone out there, you still never stopped getting me to look six times before I made a move."

"It wasn't that bad . . . was it?"

Sean looked up at the night sky and tried to focus on the half of the moon that glowed overhead. "Just at the start. But I remember it like it was yesterday. Everyone else in Briar treated me like some kind of hero from a yellowback novel, but you wouldn't leave me alone. Al-

ways asking if I was sure I was doing the right thing.
Handing out advice like you were . . ." He paused just
then so he could look back at Clint. ". . . like you were
my brother."

Nudging Sean with his elbow, Clint laughed once and
said, "Don't get too emotional on me. I thought I could
help you out at the time. There's not a whole lot of people
who would know what you might go through."

"Takes a legend to know one, huh?"

"I wouldn't have put it quite so dramatically, but you
might say it was something like that."

A silence settled between them as they both took a few
moments to think back to various points in their past. It
wasn't too late, but the town already felt as though it had
gone to sleep. Clint had done his best to steer Sean away
from the saloon district when they'd taken their walk, and
even though he wasn't too familiar with Lumley, it had
been easy enough to find the darker, quieter section.

In fact, Clint realized he'd done an extremely good job,
since they found themselves in a place that not only
seemed asleep, but completely dead. There were no places
for lanterns to be hung and not a single window glowing
within eyeshot. The only sounds to be heard were the
blowing of the wind and the occasional dog barking in
the distance.

"How did you know?" Sean asked, finally breaking the
silence.

"Know what?"

"Back then . . . in Briar. How did you know what was
going to happen to me?"

"I'm surprised you even have to ask that question,"
Clint said. "Having a name that everyone recognizes is
something I'm pretty familiar with. I've met up with a lot
of famous men and have seen plenty of them burn out
way too soon. I'd always wondered what would happen
if someone knew where they might be headed when it all

got started. And when I saw what happened to you . . . along with how everyone reacted . . . I knew you might just be getting started yourself."

"I never knew it was going to wind up like this," Sean said softly. "If I'd known . . . I never would have killed those men. I would have—"

"You would have been dead, Sean," Clint interrupted. "You know that just as well as I do. If those men had lived, they would have made sure you didn't . . . that's all there is to it. You didn't have a choice."

Sean's face became grim. Even though he sat in the darkness, he looked as though a shadow had passed over him, which turned the shadows around him into inky ghosts clawing at his heart. "There's always a choice. But not for me. Not anymore."

SIXTEEN

Lara had walked out of the cathouse where she worked, stormed down the street and charged into the Charleston Saloon before she even realized that she wasn't wearing any shoes. Having been in such a hurry to leave after what happened with Sean Albright, she was too angry to concern herself with such things as how she looked.

Ignoring all the looks she was getting from customers and workers alike, she headed straight for a table in the back where a solitary man sat facing the opposite direction. Once she was there, she walked around the table and stared down at the man with her hands propped on her hips.

"Where the hell have you been?" she asked in a grating voice.

The man ignored her at first, finding more of interest in the colored snifter he held between two fingers as though he was sitting in a plush estate. He swirled the brandy around and lifted it to his nose before finally glancing up at Lara. Without saying a word, he took a sip and looked away.

The anger inside Lara swelled up until she thought she was about to burst. She reached out, grabbed the man by the shoulder and tried to turn him around to face her. But even using all of her strength wasn't enough to get the man to budge. Even more upset by now, she instead stomped around to once again be in the man's sight.

"Don't you dare ignore me, Red. Not after everything that's happened tonight!"

Although he was called Red by just about everyone who knew him, the man didn't have a single spot of red on him. His hair was well trimmed and a shiny black color reminiscent of a raven's wing. His aristocratic face, contoured by near-perfect bone structure, seemed to have been created wearing a snooty expression, complete with a thin-lipped smile below a drooping mustache.

His nickname hadn't come from anything that could be seen. Instead, it referred to the color of the blood on his hands after killing no fewer than twenty-eight men. There were actually many more deaths to his name, but those twenty-eight were the only ones he cared about. At least another fifteen or twenty had been killed, but they were only family members or friends of the men he'd been after at the time. Ironically enough, it was those nameless innocents that gave Red Maddox his name and reputation.

Watching Lara with obvious amusement, Maddox reached up and took her hand in a solid grip. She tried to pull away, but that only made him hold on tighter until she started to squirm and grimace in pain.

"You're hurting me," she said in a fierce whisper.

The expression on Maddox's face didn't change. He kept hold of her while kicking the chair next to him away from the table with one boot. "If you didn't want to feel a little pain, you might have thought a bit more before raising your voice like that," he said with a subtle Louisiana drawl. "Maybe next time you'll remember who you're speakin' to."

Lara started to reply, but she soon found herself being dragged toward the chair and shoved forcefully back into it. When her bottom hit the seat, her wrist came free from Maddox's hand. She immediately pulled her arm in close and rubbed the spot that still ached from sharp, shooting pains. "Sorry," she said without the first hint of sincerity.

"That's quite all right. Now, would you like to talk calmly about what happened?" His eyes roamed over her body, lingering on the neckline of her cotton slip and the tumbled mess of her hair. "Judging strictly on appearances, I'd say things with Mr. Albright didn't go all too well." The way he said Sean's name sounded more like "Awl-bright" and the word slid off his tongue as though it had been greased.

"As if you didn't know . . . things went terribly. That man of yours was late and then he couldn't even get the job done."

"Since you barely have any clothes on, I trust you didn't have any trouble doin' your job?"

Lara grinned sarcastically and crossed her arms over her chest. She didn't seem ashamed of her body; she just didn't seem to want Maddox looking at it. "No. I didn't."

"Ah, that's right. You never had much of a problem in that department, did you? I've even noticed a certain . . . eagerness to please whenever Mr. Albright is concerned." Maddox's eyes fixed on her like he was a wolf trying to decide which piece to rip off first. "Am I wrong?"

"Sean got away," Lara said, completely ignoring the question posed to her. "He nearly killed me before taking off."

Maddox took another leisurely sip of his brandy. "I doubt that very much," he said. "He either killed you or he let you go. There is no 'nearly' involved. Not with one like him, anyway."

"He also took the money. *My* money."

Looking away from his glass for a moment, Maddox glanced back at Lara just long enough to peer through her like she was a dirty window. Amused with what he saw, he started to laugh quietly to himself. "That's rather . . . unexpected of him."

"The bastard even took the money he paid me for entertaining him."

Now Maddox's laughter bubbled up inside of him before spilling out in a wave that shook his shoulders and nearly brought tears to his eyes. "Oh, my lord," he said once he managed to get a hold of himself. "Now that is truly rich."

Unable to take any more of him, Lara jumped to her feet, cocked her hand back and lashed out to slap him across his face.

Maddox's left hand, which had been resting on his lap the entire time so far, now moved in a blur of motion. He lifted it straight out and up, wielding a nicely polished cane tipped with a carved silver handle. The cane cut through the air with a deep slicing sound, impacting against Lara's wrist with a sharp crack.

She recoiled and grabbed for her hand, realizing instantly that her wrist had been broken. Knowing better than to say any of the things she was thinking, Lara glared across the table at Maddox with tears leaking from the corners of her eyes.

"Sit down before you make an even bigger spectacle of yourself," he said. "I've got one more job for you."

SEVENTEEN

Any doubt that Clint might have had about Sean's sobriety was quickly dispelled when he saw the look in his friend's eyes. The last words he'd spoken still hung in the air, rattling both of their eardrums. Whatever was going through Sean's mind was enough to push aside every last bit of whiskey that had been clouding it. He now looked at Clint with perfect clarity . . . almost as though he'd already seen his own future.

"What do you mean you don't have a choice?" Clint asked. He tried not to be affected by the sudden change in Sean's temperament, but it would have been easier to simply decide not to get wet when the rain started to fall. "Of course you have a choice. If you don't like the way your life is going, you can change it. Believe me, I should know all about that."

"It's too late for me," Sean said. "I missed my one chance to keep from heading down this road." Turning to look down at his feet, he added, "I should have listened to you when I had the chance."

"Is this about your drinking?"

Smiling, Sean shook his head. "That's not the problem."

Clint felt like there was a fuse burning inside of him. And at this moment, that fuse crackled along its last few inches, carrying the spark straight into the powder keg. "Look," he said while standing up and walking around to the other side of the water trough, "I think I've been more than patient with you. I've dodged punches thrown at me for no good reason, and I've listened to you babble on like an idiot for the last couple of hours. The least you can do in return is tell me what the hell is going on here."

"You've seen me at the bottom of the heap," Sean replied. "I don't know what the hell else you want."

"Well, for starters, you could tell me what made you dive face-first into a bottle."

"Every man drinks now and then."

"Drinking is one thing. You were drowning back there and don't try to tell me any different. Hell, I haven't seen anyone pour that much into himself since I spent a night playing cards with Doc Holliday."

Sean's eyes lit up just a little bit when he heard that. "Really? How is ol' Doc nowadays?"

"He's dying. You looking to join him?"

Although he still kept his eyes focused on Clint, all of the lightheartedness quickly drained from Sean's face. "Doc may have been a bit extreme, but sometimes I wonder if he had the right idea living the way he did."

He started to say something, but Clint was stopped by one of Sean's raised hands.

"Before you say it," Sean interrupted. "I know I'm drinking more. I'm just surprised you never drank more than you did."

"This whole conversation is giving me a headache, Sean. Maybe coming to Lumley was a bad idea."

But if Sean heard Clint say that, he sure didn't give any indication. Instead, he simply blinked once and kept right on going as though nobody else had spoken a word. "I hear about you all the time from folks all over the country. And when I hear them talk, I wonder if they say half as many good things about me. But you know what the real problem is? I'm too damn busy fighting for my life every other second to get much of a chance to pay attention to the simple things. How is it that you get to listen, Clint? Don't you ever just want to sit somewhere quiet and just . . . be . . . still for a while? Don't you ever feel like you're gonna burst if you don't find some way to get some time to yourself? I mean, men like us can never just live our lives the way we want.

"So if I started drinking here and there, it's my right, isn't it? After that day, everything in the world seemed to go so fast. Just because of some rumors that spread about me, which turned into stories, until it all got so . . . out of hand. Don't you ever just want to stop everything for a little while?"

Clint nodded. "Sure. But we can't do that."

"I know. But at least I can slow it down for a while. I thought about moving around . . . just to get away from Briar. I hoped I might get someplace where they hadn't heard of me. It almost worked, too. But then it fell apart. My new life got turned on its ear. Folks got a look at the life I was tryin' to leave behind and then they started to talk about me. After that . . . it was all over. Time to move on again."

Clint thought back to the men he'd seen outside of town. Those locals had shot at him for merely mentioning Sean's name, and Clint still had no idea why. Something told him, however, that this was still not the right time to answer that particular question. "Maybe it's time to move on now."

For a moment, it seemed as though Sean had fallen into another quiet spell and wasn't about to shake himself free of it. He stared up at the sky as if he was watching something that only he could see. Whatever it was, it faded before too long and he suddenly looked up at Clint to ask, "Will they ever stop coming?"

Although Clint had been expecting a lot of different responses to his proposition, this was not one of them. If not for the deadly serious look in Sean's eyes, he might have even thought the whiskey was doing the talking again. "I don't understand."

"Sure you do. You've got to remember the first time I asked you that. I must say, you seemed better prepared for it that time around, which I suppose doesn't make the prospect of getting an answer any better."

Listening to Sean talk about it, Clint actually did start to recall hearing that question before. Just when he thought he might have nailed down the specifics, the answer pulled away just far enough to remain out of reach.

Suddenly, that same answer decided to change direction and hit him square between the eyes.

"Oh my god," he said. "I remember."

Sean nodded as a fond smile drifted over his face. "Yeah. I thought you might."

EIGHTEEN

Although he knew that one shooting in Briar was impressive, Clint figured that wouldn't be enough to do all the damage he'd been talking about to Sean. It took more than that to get a reputation started. The only thing that bothered him, however, was that Sean seemed more than eager to get more of what he'd started.

A hell of a lot more.

Two days after his fight with Mike and the men who'd made the bad decision to stand at his side, Sean was still in Briar. Clint was there as well, sticking around on the assumption that the whole situation with the murders in the area wasn't really over. Something in his gut told him that the word of a crooked sheriff was worth less than the air it floated on, and he was just about to get proof of that for himself.

Sean had been trying to get on with his normal life. Going about his business and talking to the same friends and neighbors, he was able to act as though nothing much had happened, even though knowledge of the contrary festered deep inside his brain. When he talked with Clint, Sean commented on how much he valued his advice, but he didn't think it truly fit the situation.

Clint had listened and stopped trying to say anything else to him on the subject. All the while, he hoped that at least something of what he'd told him had stuck. And if nothing else happened, he figured that those same warnings would simply fade away and this whole ordeal would just be a colorful memory.

Those hopes lasted for two days.

They were shattered the moment Clint saw Sean charging toward him, a look of anger burning on his young features.

"That son of a bitch!" Sean snarled. "That lying, cowardly son of a bitch!"

Passing the time at a game of poker, Clint sat facing the door to the local saloon that had become his favorite spot in Briar. The stakes never got too high and the company was always good. On this day, he'd been watching the door with a bad feeling festering in his gut. At that moment, he knew exactly where that feeling had come from.

"What's wrong?" Clint asked while tossing his cards down and getting to his feet. "Who are you talking about?"

"The sheriff. After all he told us he still—"

Clint cut him off by grabbing the front of his jacket and hauling him out the door. Once they were outside, he tossed Sean almost into the side of the saloon.

"What the hell is that about?" Sean asked as his hands balled up into fists.

"I was just about to ask you the same thing. You don't go stomping around like some angry kid, shooting your mouth off about the sheriff like that."

"But he's crooked."

"We don't have real proof of that. But if he is, that's exactly why you can't be heard talking like that." Clint stared at Sean intently, the initial tension between them bleeding off like heat from a dying fire.

"You're right, Clint." Now Sean seemed extra careful to look around and study where he was and who else was around. "But I heard that the sheriff and some of his deputies are gonna take another stagecoach coming in from the Dakota territories."

Clint's eyes flashed with anger. This time, he was almost the one to forget himself and start shouting. "What?" The sharp sound of his voice caught his attention and he quickly quieted down again. "How did you find out about this?"

"A friend of mine, Charlie Wagner, told me. One of the deputies is his cousin, and he heard the kid bragging about how rich they was gonna be and that not even two gunfighters had enough to stop them."

Taking a deep breath, Clint felt the blood pounding through his chest and his lungs swelling like bellows. What angered him the most was the smug look that had been on the sheriff's face when he'd talked to them last. Clint just knew that the lawman had been smiling at them knowing the whole time that he was going to walk all over them and do whatever the hell he wanted to do, no matter how many people had to die along the way.

"I guess that's our proof. Which stage is it?" he asked.

Sean stepped in closer, lowering his voice almost to a whisper. "Should be rolling into town around six. They're carrying a payroll that's on its way to a railroad office in Iowa."

"Passengers?"

"Does it matter?" Sean asked.

Clint looked over to the younger man just then with a new respect. He could see in Sean's face that he wasn't like some of the others that were naturals with a gun. He wasn't eager to pick fights just because he knew he could win them, and he wasn't about to charge into any conflict just to get an excuse to test his newly discovered skills.

This one had promise, Clint thought.

He wasn't in the practice of tracking down gunmen at the start of his career, but he did know one when he saw one. The first time he'd seen one, Clint never said a word, figuring it best to simply let the kid go about his life however he wanted.

Eighteen months later, Clint met up with that same kid again. Only this time, he was trying to make a name for himself by testing his iron against the best. Clint had been the best . . . and he'd also been the one to send that kid to his grave.

Ever since then, Clint had wondered if he could have steered that kid in another direction by giving him just a few friendly words of advice. He was testing that theory now. So far, it seemed to be coming along nicely.

Nodding, Clint said, "You're right. It doesn't matter. After all we've seen, it's safe to say that whoever is on that stage will be killed unless something's done about it."

Sean's face shone with eagerness. He nodded quickly as his hand dropped to rest on the handle of his pistol. "You mean unless *we* do something about it."

"Yeah. That's exactly what I mean."

NINETEEN

After finding out where the stagecoach would be coming in—from the relief driver waiting for it in Briar—Clint and Sean headed out of town to meet it as quickly as their horses could carry them. Between both of the animals, the ride went even faster than they'd expected, and it wasn't too long before Clint caught sight of something on a ridge less than a mile in the distance.

Holding his hand up, Clint reined Duke to a stop. Sean pulled up alongside him. "There they are," Clint said, pointing to a cloud of dust being kicked up in the distance.

Once the horses had stopped, it was easy enough to hear the stage's team pounding against the ground. The rattle of the coach and the jangle of the animals' gear rode on the wind to announce their presence.

"Sounds like they're still riding at full speed," Sean said.

"They must know about all of the trouble in this area. I'll bet they even have a pretty heavy guard on board to protect their cargo."

"The sheriff must know about that, too."

"Exactly what I was thinking." Snapping his reins,

Clint leaned down low into the wind as Duke took off running. "Come on."

Sean didn't miss a beat and was at Clint's side again after less than a few seconds' worth of catching up. Between their horses and the ones pulling the stagecoach, Clint and Sean met up with their target in no time at all.

Sure enough, there were twice the normal number of men riding shotgun, one sitting next to the stage's driver and another perched behind him. Both of these men brought their guns to bear on Clint the moment they saw that they were no longer alone on the dusty stretch of road.

Clint slowed Duke to a walk and lifted his hands in the air. "We're here to help," he said.

When the driver saw Sean coming up beside Clint, he knew he couldn't steer the coach safely around both of them without taking the risk of rolling off the trail. And with a fairly steep ditch on either side of the trail, leading to a slope into rough terrain, driving off the beaten path was not much of an option for anything that relied on wheels instead of four strong legs. With this in mind, the driver pulled back of his own reins and eventually stopped the coach.

By this time, both of the shotgunners had their weapons trained on Clint and Sean. Besides them, another pair of riflemen stuck their heads out from the coach's passenger compartment.

"What the hell do you want?" asked the shotgunner next to the driver.

Sean put his hand on Clint's shoulder as he went by, saying, "I've got this one."

Clint nodded and let Sean take control.

"I'm Sean Albright and I worked with the posse that's been on patrol since the robberies started."

Both the shotgunner and the driver leaned forward in their seats and squinted intently. Once they got a good look, they eased up somewhat and lowered their guard just a bit. "We heard'a you," the driver said.

"We know there's going to be some trouble here," Sean continued. "So my friend and I thought we'd escort you the rest of the way into town."

The driver smiled at that. "Sounds fine to me," he said, leaning back in his seat as though a weight had been lifted off his shoulders. "We'd appreciate any help you can offer. But where's the sheriff? I thought he'd be out to meet them killers himself."

Sean choked back what he truly wanted to say, deciding to go for the quick solution and deal with the ugly truth when there was more time. "He's around. Right now we just need to get you and your men into—"

"Oh, he's around, all right," came a voice from behind the stage. "In fact, he's right here."

At that moment, the shotgunners turned to look as the sheriff and four of his men rode their horses into a semicircle around the stagecoach. The driver raised his hand in greeting and started to say something to the lawman. But before he could get one word out, the air was suddenly full of smoky explosions as a hail of lead tore through the stage as well as the men riding it.

Clint had reflexively drawn his Colt when he'd seen the sheriff, but couldn't get a clear shot from where he was positioned. When he looked around to try and see what Sean was doing, he couldn't find a trace of the other man. All that was left was a cloud of dust kicked up by his horse.

The first man to fall was the shotgunner perched on the back of the stage. He'd brought his weapon up to his shoulder, but didn't manage to get his finger clamped on the trigger before no fewer than half a dozen bullets lifted him to his feet and pitched him down to the ground.

Although his instincts had been to seek cover before facing the shooters, the shotgunner next to the driver had only the thin wood of the bench to protect him. That stopped enough of the bullets to buy him some time to shoot back, but only once. His shotgun thundered among the rest of the gunfire half a second before the first round tore through his arm. Another shot grazed his shoulder and then three more found his chest.

Dropping down off of Duke, Clint kept his head low and dashed toward the stage, trying to keep the coach between himself and as many of the gunmen as possible. Even so, a couple of the sheriff's men were able to put him cleanly in their sights and it was they who were Clint's first targets.

Not worrying about any fire coming his way, Clint charged straight toward the gunmen. In fact, he'd been hoping to draw some of the killers' attention away from the stage and onto himself. At least that would give whatever passengers were inside the coach a brief opportunity to seek some cover.

"Over here!" Clint shouted as he ran.

That caught the attention of the gunman closest to him. As soon as Clint saw that man turning to face him, he pointed the Colt and squeezed the trigger. It bucked against his palm one time only, but that was more than enough to drop the killer to the dirt.

Clint shifted his aim to the second gunman in his sight, but was unable to fire before his target ducked behind the coach quicker than a rabbit with its tail on fire. Instead of chasing after that one, Clint hopped up onto the stage to see what he could do for the driver.

Bullets flew through the air like a swarm of wasps, whipping around with a deadly hissing noise that set every one of Clint's nerves on end. He could see the stagecoach driver hunched down between the bench and the front edge of the coach, both hands clasped tightly over his head.

"Are you all right?" Clint asked as he reached out for the terrified man.

The driver didn't move. Clint's first thought was that the man was already dead, but his hopes returned when he saw the driver peek out from behind his knotted fingers.

Bending down close to him, Clint repeated his question and this time he got a hurried nod in response. "Can you move?"

"Hell yes, just give me a chance to get off this thing."

"You've got it, now go!"

And with that, Clint jumped down from the stage just as two of the sheriff's men came walking around from the other end. Clint lifted the Colt and let loose with a volley of bullets that sent the killers scrambling for cover as the driver rushed away in the opposite direction.

Clint took a quick look over his shoulder to check on the driver as his fingers worked at reloading the Colt. "Couldn't leave well enough alone, Sheriff?" he asked to buy himself a few more seconds.

But there was no response.

Snapping the cylinder shut, Clint looked around for Sean and couldn't find him, either. At that moment, he heard another wave of gunfire coming from around the other side of the stage. Clint fought back his instinct to head for cover and instead ran toward the stage door, praying that he could get the passengers out alive.

TWENTY

More than anything, Sean couldn't stand a man who lied right to his face and expected to get away with it. The moment he'd heard the sheriff's voice, he pictured the crooked lawman's face, laughing as he went against his word and destroyed as many lives as he damn well pleased.

Sean wasn't about to stand by and let anyone else get hurt. Not after so many others had been killed already. Not even if he had to put his own life on the line to stop it.

As he rode toward the stage, he didn't even pay attention to the sound of gunfire echoing through his ears. He simply spurred his horse to move as fast as it could until he was in sight of the biggest group of the gunmen. From there, he'd lifted himself up in the saddle and jumped onto the first shooter he could see, even as the other man swung around and took a shot at him out of sheer reflex.

Letting out a primal scream, Sean dropped onto the gunman as though he'd been shot from a cannon, taking both himself and his target off their feet. The gunshots still raged around him as he drove his fist into the gunman's face. Acting more out of panic than anything else, the gunman lifted his hand up to aim his pistol at the side of Sean's head.

Sean caught sight of that at the last possible second, batting away the other man's weapon with the butt of his own pistol. The bones in the gunman's wrist shattered, and before he could cry out in pain, his mouth was full of the barrel of Sean's gun. One second later, the contents of his skull were blasted into the ground beneath him.

Pulling back the hammer as he got to his feet, Sean looked up just as the sheriff himself came striding into view. The lawman wore a smug grin that set Sean's blood on fire. But before he could fire off another round, Sean felt something hit the small of his back like a battering ram.

The sky and ground tilted crazily in Sean's vision as he was knocked almost out his boots by another one of the sheriff's men. Sean tried to twist himself around to get a look at the one who'd tackled him, but only managed to see the glint of sunlight against metal as a pistol was shoved suddenly into his face.

Sean didn't think to question his instincts as his body naturally pulled to one side just as a gunshot thundered less than a foot away from him. He could hear the bullet thump into the ground after whipping past his face, the sound reminding him of a club slapping against a sack of grain.

But Sean was too focused to be rattled by the near miss. Instead, his mind could only push him forward toward his goal of reaching the sheriff. And with that in mind, the man who'd nearly blown his head off became nothing but an obstacle in his way.

Sean shook him off and charged forward. All he needed to see was a hint of motion coming from behind for him to pivot at the waist, aim and fire. His bullet caught the gunman who'd tackled him square in the chest. Sean didn't even bother to look and see the man fall. He simply knew the bullet had struck home.

The sheriff watched all of this with an amused grin. That expression melted from his face, however, when he saw that Sean was still coming, even after all the attempts that had been made to put him down. Steeling himself as Sean approached, the crooked lawman held his gun at waist level and cocked back the hammer.

"You can let this go," the sheriff said. "Let it go and we can part ways without any bad blood between us."

Sean came to a stop less than ten feet from where the sheriff was standing. "Even after watching your men die?"

"That's business. I'm sure even someone like you could understand that a businessman doesn't let his personal feelings get in the way of things."

Shaking his head, Sean gripped his pistol so tightly that his knuckles became white around its handle. "You had your chance to walk away, but you decided to ignore it."

The sheriff simply shrugged. "No profit in walking away. Besides, if you're all I have to worry about, then I don't see much use in turning away from a good payday. This way's fine with me."

"Finally we agree on something."

Both men stared at each other for the next several seconds. Although less than a minute passed, they seemed to glare across at one another for an eternity. Both of their weapons were already drawn, but each one knew that the slightest move on his part would unleash all the hell they had in store for each other.

Listening for any more of the sheriff's men, Sean could hear the sounds of a struggle coming from the other side of the stagecoach. He knew Clint was still over there and became anxious to make sure he was doing all right. But on the other hand, he knew better than to rush his standoff with the lawman since that was exactly the type of thing the sheriff would be waiting for.

At that moment, Sean heard the frightened voice of a woman passenger, followed by the sound of a single gunshot. Sean's mind filled with images of more dead innocents, or even the possibility that Clint himself could be hurt—all because Sean hadn't been there just a few seconds sooner.

That was more than enough to push Sean into action. The instant the muscles in his gun arm started to flex, both men knew the fight was underway.

First, Sean centered his aim on the sheriff, doing his best to make a killing shot from the hip. A fraction of a second after that, the sheriff lifted his pistol and squeezed his trigger.

A single shot punched through the air between them, drilling a messy hole through the sheriff's brain.

The lawman's eyes widened in surprise. His arm dropped to his side as his finger clenched around the trigger. His gun discharged harmlessly into the ground, the hole it made soon covered up when his body dropped on top of it.

But Sean didn't wait to watch the other man's fall. He was already stepping up to the stagecoach, hoping that he wasn't too late to be any help to those inside.

TWENTY-ONE

It was all Clint could do to force himself not to worry too much about what Sean was doing or where he'd taken off to. They'd come out to meet the stage to do their best and save the people on board, so that had to be Clint's top priority. After all he'd seen, Clint also figured that Sean was more than able to take care of himself.

Clint grabbed hold of the handle to the door of the coach and looked through the window. The first thing he saw was the bloody body of one of the riflemen slumped back in his seat, his face devastated from one of the gunmen's bullets.

Huddled on the floor, there were two women, an older man and the last rifleman. Although they all looked terrified, one of the women stared up at Clint with wide, brown eyes.

He didn't have time to ask if anyone else was hurt. All Clint could do was look them over quickly to see if he could spot any major wounds or pools of blood. Not finding any on the survivors, Clint was about to move on when he heard movement coming from his right side.

Out of the corner of his eye, he spotted another of the sheriff's men trying to work his way behind him. Before the killer could take another step, Clint tightened his grip on the stage's door and swung it open as hard as he could. The edge of the door caught the killer on the bridge of his nose and in moments, his face was drenched with blood.

Clint followed up the first strike with a straight left jab to the other man's jaw. He rattled the killer's entire head with the blow while still keeping himself ready for any retaliation coming his way.

The killer staggered back half a step, but managed to bring up his pistol and thumb back the hammer.

Spotting the move with plenty of time to spare, Clint grabbed hold of the other man's wrist and pointed the gun skyward just before it went off. After dropping the Colt into its holster, he pushed the killer back and punched him again, this time driving his fist slightly higher than before so he could pound the guy again in the nose.

Cartilage snapped beneath his knuckles, buying Clint another second or two for him to finish the killer off. Knowing full well how much pain came with a broken nose, Clint turned quickly toward the coach and said, "Quick, get out of there!"

The passengers seemed rooted to their spots, however. Even the rifleman seemed too scared to do more than stare blankly back at him. Before Clint could give them another order, the woman with the brown eyes suddenly pointed toward Clint and let out a panicked scream.

Instinctively, Clint spun around to look and was just in time to spot the killer with the broken nose as he struggled through the pain to bring his pistol up to bear. The other man's gun was nearly on target when Clint snapped the Colt from his side and pulled the trigger.

The only thing registering on the killer's face was complete shock. It was impossible to say whether he was more surprised at the speed of Clint's draw or the fact that a bullet had just passed through his body. That last bit of knowledge would pass into the great beyond right along with the man who possessed it, as the killer dropped first to his knees and then onto his face.

Clint then turned to look through the windows of the stagecoach, hoping to see through the other side. All he could make out was the blur of movement and a gout of smoke as a pair of gunshots echoed in the stagnant air. He waited for a second or two, unsure if there were any more gunmen to worry about.

But a heavy silence descended upon the scene. It was the kind of total quiet that settled onto a battlefield once the last of the shots had been fired, leaving only the victors and corpses to survey what was left behind. Clint took a quick look around before holstering the Colt once again.

The passengers were just starting to feel safe enough to glance about themselves.

They all seemed healthy at first, despite the sickened expressions that came onto their faces when they saw the body of the rifleman on the seat next to them. Clint opened the door and reached inside toward the passengers.

"Is anyone else hurt?" he asked.

Before he could get a reply, Clint saw a figure lunge toward the opposite window. His hand went reflexively for his gun, but he stopped himself once he realized it was only Sean peeking in from the other side.

Clint looked across at Sean and asked, "How many more of them are there?"

"No more. What about you?"

"I got the ones over here. Come around and help get these people out of this carriage."

The passengers were more than happy to get into the fresh air. Once they truly realized they were out of danger, they started to talk nervously among themselves. Clint and Sean pulled the rifleman's body from the compartment and lowered it onto the ground.

"What about the sheriff?" Clint asked. "Did he get away?"

Sean didn't even have to shake his head. The solemn look in his eyes told Clint everything he needed to know.

Clint patted Sean on the shoulder. "You did a real good job out here."

"Tell that to those shotgunners," Sean replied while looking up to the bodies which still sat slumped on top of the stage. "Tell them how good a job I did."

"You did your best. That's all anyone can be expected to—"

Clint was cut off by the surviving rifleman, who walked straight up to Sean and grabbed hold of his hand. "I saw it all," he said while shaking Sean's hand as though he was working a water pump. "Those men had you dead to rights. They had us all and you gunned 'em down like they weren't even there!"

Although the rifleman glanced back and forth between Sean and Clint, he seemed to be transfixed by Sean. The look on his face was something close to reverence. "If I hadn't seen it with my own eyes, I'd have never believed it." Leaning in a little closer, he asked, "You . . . you're Sean Albright, aren't you?"

Sean nodded.

Now the rifleman's eyes widened to the size of saucers. "I heard about you, all right! Hot damn!" When he pulled his hand back, the rifleman looked down at it as though he'd managed to touch an angel's wing. He hurried back to the other passengers and told them of his discovery in an excited whisper.

TWENTY-TWO

Sean simply watched the passengers with a mixture of confusion and annoyance. Turning to Clint, he said, "I didn't know what you were talking about before when you were telling me what people say and what could happen after that. But now I know . . . you were right. He looked at me like I was a hero or something."

"You'll probably just have to get used to that," Clint said. "It looks like they might build you a statue when you get back to town. They might even petition to name the place after you."

Smiling sarcastically, Sean gave Clint a short, humorless laugh. "I'm serious, Clint."

"So am I. What do you like better? Sean's Junction or maybe Albright Pass?"

But Clint's attempts to lighten the mood were having no effect. And although he was most definitely kidding about some of what he was saying, Clint knew that a little piece of it was turning out to be true. That became especially clear when all of the passengers looked over at Sean with the same kind of reverence in their eyes.

"We've both been through a lot today," Clint said.

"Let's just get these folks back to Briar and collect on the
free drinks that they'd better offer us."

Now that truly did seem to brighten Sean's mood. He
nodded and walked over to the stagecoach while Clint
pulled the bodies off from the top of the wagon. They
decided to unhitch the team from their bridles and ride
back into town on the horses, leaving the coach to be
found by a fresh group of men who'd clean up and survey
the damage.

Clint made sure to take the lockbox from beneath the
driver's seat and made it his personal duty to deliver it
into the proper hands. While they were riding back into
town, Clint watched Sean closely. The other man seemed
to be taking his victory as though it had been anything
but. His head hung low and he moved slower than normal
even though he didn't have a scratch on him.

But the stagecoach's rifleman didn't seem to notice that
one bit. All the way back to Briar, he kept talking about
the gunfight and what a sight it had been to witness Sean
in action. The only person besides Clint that wasn't completely enraptured by the story was the brown-eyed
woman, who seemed perfectly happy to keep her eyes on
Clint.

It took less than a couple of hours for the word to spread
through town about what had happened with the sheriff.
Roughly a half hour after that, the story began to grow,
until Sean Albright was being regarded as the fastest gun
this side of the Mississippi River.

Soon, there was a party being thrown in his honor and
everyone in town wanted to buy him a drink, shake his
hand, or just be in his presence for a few minutes. There
was so much merriment in Briar that even Sean had a
hard time keeping his spirits down. In no time at all, the
smile on his face was nearly enough to light up the saloon,
long after the sun had dipped below the horizon.

By midnight, the number of people at the celebration was thinning out, but the party was a far cry from being over. Sean and Clint were drinking together, swapping bawdy stories, when they both took a moment to absorb what was going on around them.

"Can you believe all of this?" Sean asked.

Clint grinned and downed the rest of his beer. "Come on, Sean. Everyone's been hearing about, and seeing, an awful lot of death lately. They finally have some good news to talk about, so they throw a party. Sounds like as good a reason as any."

"Sure, but . . . all the things they've been saying. About me, I mean. Isn't it all a bit . . . much?"

"You should only worry when they start saying bad things. And if I know you well enough, they'll have plenty of chances for nasty rumors later. If it makes you feel any better, I can start one right now."

Sean laughed and set his glass on the bar. As soon as the barkeep saw it there, he brought over a bottle and topped it off again, accepting only a polite wave as payment.

Just as Sean was about to say something else, a thundering crash shook through the saloon. It sounded as though the building was coming down, but when they turned to look, Clint and Sean spotted a local standing over a busted table.

People scattered away from the young man as he lifted another chair over his head and slammed it down onto the same spot as the one he'd used to break the table. "You ain't nothin', Albright," he shouted in a drunken slur. "Nothin' but a punk that got lucky. An' that's all you'll ever be."

Sean squinted through the haze that had settled into his own eyes after too much alcohol. "Jack? What're you talking about?"

"Yeah," grunted the stagecoach rifleman who now sat

in the corner closest to the front door. "Shut yer mouth, Jack, before Sean teaches you a lesson in manners!"

Raising his hands, Sean started to say, "No, no. I wouldn't—" but he was suddenly drowned in a wave of shouted insults directed toward the local who'd started it all.

Clint recognized the look in Jack's eyes well enough. He'd seen it countless times before and it never led to anything but trouble. Reaching out to steady Sean before he made a move, Clint said, "If there's a problem, maybe you'd like to take it up with me."

Jack barely regarded Clint with more than a passing glance. "I got no business with you. It's him I came to see," he said, pointing to Sean.

"Go ahead and say what you want to say," Sean demanded.

Grinning slightly, Jack straightened up and squared his shoulders. "There's a lot of talk going on about you. Some of us are sick of it."

"Then don't listen."

"I think I'd rather see how much of it is true for myself. Personally, I think it ain't nothing but a load of bullshit."

The stage driver had been keeping to himself for most of the night. Now he stood up and shouted in a voice full of confidence, "Teach him a lesson, Sean! He's got it coming."

"Yeah," Jack said as his hand drifted toward his gun. "Teach me that lesson."

TWENTY-THREE

"You don't have to do this," Clint whispered.

But Sean wouldn't so much as take his eyes from the man who'd decided to challenge him. For a moment, it was uncertain as to whether or not he'd even heard what Clint had said. But just as Clint was about to repeat himself, Sean replied, "Yes, I do, Clint. And you know it."

Clint did know it. The snowball had already started rolling down the mountain and it was too late to get rid of it now. If anybody else stepped in, Sean would be branded a coward and all these fair-weather friends would disappear at best, possibly turn on him at worst. Besides, Clint also knew that Sean wouldn't even entertain the thought of someone fighting his battles.

Clint knew all of this, but that didn't mean he had to like it.

Rather than argue with the younger man, Clint stepped aside. Still, he made sure to be ready in case his help was needed after all.

"So go ahead," Jack prodded. "Teach me my lesson. Or are those stories I heard about you bullshit, after all?"

Sean's face turned to stone. His eyes bored into Jack like a drill, but he still didn't make a move for his gun.

The two stood facing each other for half a minute, the space between them cleared away by the others inside the saloon itching to see a fight. Clint watched alongside the stagecoach's rifleman, noticing that everyone in the place acted as though they were about to see a show rather than something that may end one or both of the participants' lives.

Before too long, it became obvious that Sean wasn't about to make the first move. Sensing this, Jack started to become anxious, which was the worst possible mistake he could have made. The muscles in his face started tugging at the corner of his right eye. His fingers began wriggling over the handle of his gun and his tongue darted out to wet his lips as if in preparation for a good meal.

Finally, Jack's face took on an expression of commitment to forging ahead, whatever the consequences may be. Clint recognized that look as the one that came right before the draw, and he hoped that Sean could read it just as well.

Jack's hand closed around his pistol and he pulled it from his holster in a stiff, hurried motion. The end of the barrel snagged on the holster's lip, but he wrenched it free and thumbed back the hammer.

Taking all of this in, Sean let out the breath he'd been holding and allowed his reflexes to take over from there. He focused on nothing but his target while making a smooth draw. He cleared leather a fraction of a second after Jack, but did so with such fluidity that he managed to cock the hammer and squeeze the trigger at the same time as his opponent.

Both guns went off, filling the saloon with smoky thunder. While Jack's shot had been rushed, Sean's was careful and deliberate. The former bullet whipped through the air a few inches off target to the right, while Sean's round caught Jack in the center of his chest.

Sean paused and was about to fire again when he saw

the dark crimson stain spread on Jack's shirt.

Suddenly, all the color drained from Jack's face. Looking down, he caught sight of the stain; his hands opened up, dropping the gun to the floor as he pressed both palms to his chest. "Jesus," he rasped as he dropped to his knees. "I . . . I'm dyin'. I'm really dyin'."

Sean still held his .45 in hand as he watched the life drain out of the other man to form a blackish puddle on the floorboards. He looked around to the others inside the saloon, only to receive approving nods in return. Dropping his hand to his side, he stepped over Jack's body and walked quickly out the front door.

The moment Sean left, everyone else inside started talking excitedly once again. Clint watched them for a second or two, wondering if this was what it was like whenever he was forced to draw down on some aspiring gunfighter who was only too eager to die. Rather than think about it too long, he walked outside and looked for Sean.

It wasn't too hard to find him, since Sean was standing just across the street from the saloon. Although some of the locals were looking curiously in his direction, none of them seemed too anxious to approach him just yet. Clint walked up to him and stood at his side for a few moments before saying anything.

"That was some good shooting," Clint said finally. "Fastest I've seen in a while."

"I don't understand," Sean said quietly. "Why did he come for me? I've known that man for years. We weren't the best of friends, but he never wanted to kill me, for god's sake."

"It's what I was trying to tell you about before," Clint said, without trying to sound as if he was giving him an I-told-you-so. "Once word starts getting around about a man being the best at something, there's always going to be those who want to prove him wrong."

"But I never said I was the best."

"You didn't have to. Folks around here have been doing that for you."

"And now that I killed him?"

Taking a deep breath, Clint replied, "They'll be talking
about that, too. I wish I could've been a little more help.
I saw this coming, but didn't do too good of a job in
trying to stop it."

Sean turned to Clint with a new look in his eyes. This
time, there was no sadness or remorse. There wasn't even
a hint of regret or guilt over what had happened. All that
remained was acceptance. "For a man I met hardly a
month ago, you've done a hell of a lot for me. As for the
rest of it, I don't know what you could've done about any
of that."

"To be honest, I don't really know what I could've
done, either. It still feels strange to ride into a town and
have people know me, and it's even stranger to have them
want to kill me. When I saw what happened to you along
with everything that came after, I knew firsthand that your
life was going to change. Maybe I thought I could at least
give you a choice in the matter."

"You did, Clint. And back there, I made my choice.
Now it's up to me to see it through."

Both men thought that over for a few quiet minutes.
For the first time since his initial fight with Mike's posse,
Sean seemed to be at peace with himself and what he'd
done. Clint, too, felt as though he'd done everything he
could to put the murders straight and help Sean as much
as possible.

"I guess I'll be moving on tomorrow morning," Clint
said. "There's some friends I'd like to see in Colorado."

"I think I'll be heading out, too. If I stay here for too
much longer, I'll become a drunk with all these free
drinks that keep getting thrown at me."

Both men laughed a bit at that. When the laughter
stopped, Sean turned to Clint and asked, "You've seen

this happen a lot, haven't you? What happened to me, I mean."

"Not a lot, but a few times." Clint could see the seriousness that had once again settled into Sean's face. "It's not as bad as I made it sound. Hell, it could all blow over in a month or two. Maybe less."

"But what if it doesn't blow over? I guess what I'm trying to get at is . . . do they ever stop coming?"

Clint wasn't confused by the question, but he was thrown off a bit by it. "Who do you mean?"

"Men like Jack . . . or even the sheriff. Once they hear about you, do they ever really forget about you and leave you alone? Do they ever stop coming for you?"

Clint thought about it for a second. That very thing had been something he'd been wrestling with for a while and he'd already come to terms with the fact that it would be with him for a great while to come. As for what he should say to Sean at that point in time, he knew that his honest answer would only cause him undue worry. And since Clint doubted if he even knew the real answer anyhow, he decided to spare Sean a lot of restless nights . . . by lying to him.

"Sure, Sean. They'll stop someday."

TWENTY-FOUR

Ten years later, in another state and in a world that had changed a hell of a lot for both men, Sean was finally holding Clint responsible for the lie he'd been told back in Briar, Nebraska.

Sitting next to the horse trough with the dirty water streaming down his face, leaves stuck to his hair and the stink of alcohol drifting on his breath, Sean Albright looked Clint in the eyes and said, "You told me they would stop. You said that after a while, people would forget my name and lose interest in picking fights with me for no reason."

"I know what I told you, but—"

"You lied to me, Clint! Why?"

"Because I'm not a fortune-teller," Clint said, his voice edged with frustration. "What did you want me to say? That I know better than anybody just how far some men will go to make a name for themselves by putting a bullet through your skull? That you should get ready for a life of getting challenged by every loudmouth gunslinger in every town you go to and hearing stories that only make it worse?"

"If that was what you thought was gonna happen, then yes!"

"You were already on that road. What the hell was I supposed to do about it?"

"Let me know what I was in for, that's what."

"So I guess it's all my fault, then," Clint snapped. "Everything that happened from that day on was all my fault and if I would've told you anything different back then, your whole life would've just been one field of daisies. Is that what you want to hear?"

Sean was silent for a moment. Even though he was looking at Clint, his mind was obviously hundreds of miles and several years away.

But Clint pressed on anyway, even if he was talking just to get the words out in the open no matter who else could hear them. "Every time I heard your name after that day, I was proud to say that I knew you. And when I heard about all the men you faced and all the outlaws you brought to justice, I knew you'd gone on to become someone who deserved all the praise he got. But besides all that, I also knew how hard it was because I live with a lot of the same things as you. I know what it's like to be waiting for someone to call out my name just before they take a shot at me. And though you were going through all of that, too, I figured you were strong enough to handle it.

"So is this how you handle it now, Sean? By drowning yourself in whiskey until you can't even stand up on your own two feet? Are you trying to get yourself killed? Is that why you tear down your own name for everyone to see?"

Snapping out of his silence, Sean jumped to his feet and glared down at Clint. "And what if I am? I asked you ten years ago if they'd ever stop coming, but you didn't see fit to give me the right answer. Well, I'll give it to you right now. They *never* stop coming!"

TWENTY-FIVE

"I try to live my life like any other man," Sean said. "But there's no way to get away from who I am. I change my name, but someone always recognizes me. After I moved out of Briar, I tried to settle down and take a wife, but she only married me because she wanted to have a husband who was a known man . . . a gunfighter. She wasn't no better than the rest of them. And once she started talking to her friends about me, they started coming again like rats from the woodwork."

Sean let out a shuddering breath and dropped down to sit on the edge of the trough. He ran his fingers through his hair, grabbing it tightly as though he was about to pull it out of his head. "I tried to walk away at first. Just don't fight them and they'll leave, right? But it doesn't work that way. They want to kill you whether you fight or not, and as much as I wanted to be out of their sights, I couldn't just let them kill me.

"If I could turn it off, I would. Believe me, I would. But once it's in your blood, you can't just shake it out. Someone draws on you and you react. There's no stopping it. It just . . . happens. And the more it happens, the better you get."

Clint thought to what it felt like when he was facing another man hell-bent on killing him. Once the talking was over and the bullets started to fly, his body ran as though it didn't need him to think about what needed to be done. The reflexes carried him through to the end. They didn't need to be told what to do—and it was next to impossible to hold them back.

"Maybe it would all be different," Sean went on. "If I was half as good as they say I am . . . maybe even as good as you . . . I could change it all around. But as it is, the only way I can stop from thinking about it is to get so drunk that I can't hardly think about much at all. That made me feel better for a while . . . until my wife ran off on me and the days started flowing by without me knowing it."

"How long ago was that?" Clint asked.

"Coming up on three years ago now."

"What about San Antonio? I heard that you were down there sometime last spring and . . ." Clint paused as he recalled the story, which might have been one of Sean's more recent sore spots. "Let's just say I'd have a hard time believing you could have done any of that drunk. Were you even there? Do you know what I'm talking about?"

"Sure," Sean said while nodding slowly. "I was there. And I was drunk . . . real drunk. That gang thought they could get the drop on me by coming in all at once. Hell, even I thought they had me when I saw how many of them there were. I tried to pass myself off as someone else. Even tried walking away, but they wouldn't have none of it. I was so drunk, it was all a blur after that. When I came to, I was in a jail cell and a marshal was telling me I'd gunned down six men three days before. Said he watched me do it with his own eyes, so I guess it had to be true."

"Six men?" Clint said with genuine awe. "I heard there were only four."

"I couldn't tell you either way. Like I said . . . I was drunk."

Although Clint hated to push the man any further, he decided to ask him something that had been bothering him ever since he'd ridden into town. And since there probably wasn't going to be a truly good time for it, he figured that now was as good as ever.

"I've been hearing some other stories," Clint said. "Actually, I've only heard bits and pieces, but I've got to tell you that they're not too good."

"If you heard 'em from folks around here, then I'm not surprised in the least."

"Do you know the people that live in the big house a mile or two southwest of town?"

Sean thought about that for a second and then shook his head.

"Well, they seem to know you. In fact, they started shooting at me the moment I asked about where I could find you."

A shadow of concern drifted over Sean's face. "Did any of them make it?"

"I didn't kill any of them if that's what you're asking. They didn't seem too anxious to extend the same courtesy to me, though."

"No . . . I guess they wouldn't."

"So who were they?" When Clint saw that Sean was starting to fade out again, he grabbed hold of the man by both shoulders and made sure he had his attention. "Answer me."

But Sean was too far gone. Although the liquor no longer seemed to have a hold on him, the look in his eyes said that he was getting too tired to think straight. When he saw that, Clint started to feel his own fatigue. He grew even more tired when he realized how late it had gotten.

"The sun's going to be up soon," Clint said. "How about we get some sleep and try to start this visit over again tomorrow?"

Sean nodded weakly.

"You need any help getting back home?"

"Nah," Sean replied. "I'm used to finding my way."

Clint watched his friend walk away. The stagger was gone and so was the spring in his step. All that remained was an invisible weight which pushed on his shoulders and stooped over his back. Something in the back of Clint's mind had to wonder if he would ever see the man again.

TWENTY-SIX

Red Maddox stood outside of one of the shabbiest boarding-houses in Lumley with all the posturing of a man awaiting a visit from the queen. Despite the fact that dawn was fast approaching and his head hadn't touched a pillow in more than twenty-seven hours, he still maintained himself with complete, effortless ease. He stood leaning on his cane at the mouth of an alley next to a burned-out storefront, casually swinging his pocket watch on the end of a gold chain.

As had been true for the last hour or two, the only thing running through his mind was his meeting with Sean Albright. Of course, Albright didn't know about the meeting . . . not yet, anyway. But that just made the thought of it all the sweeter.

Red had known damn well that the men he'd sent along with that whore wouldn't be enough to finish the job. In fact, he'd been counting on it. If the likes of them could kill someone like Albright, then Albright deserved to die in a cheap brothel.

But men like him didn't deserve their lives to end in filthy places such as those. Even pathetic drunks like Albright had earned the right to be snuffed out properly. A single stutter of a laugh came to the top of Red's throat when he thought about that phrase.

Snuffed out.

It seemed so appropriate, especially when applied to a man like Albright. Red had been watching that one develop for some time, knowing that someday he would have to pay him a visit, once he became good enough to earn the right. Albright was a sputtering flame choking on its own wax, blazing brightly one second and almost fading away the next.

Flames like that were unpredictable and therefore more dangerous than any other. Just when you thought they were nothing but smoke, they would spark back to life, burning anything unfortunate to be around them at that particular moment.

Red savored the analogy for another minute or two before his eyes locked onto something moving at the other end of the street. Turning casually to look, Red immediately recognized the figure, right down to the way it dragged one foot in front of the other as though it was a man walking in his own funeral procession.

Albright.

Keeping his eye on the other man, Red took a few steps back into a shadow. He was fairly certain that he wouldn't be seen, but he made the effort to hide all the same. After all, it simply wouldn't do to get too far ahead of himself.

The first light of dawn broke through the sky just as Albright trudged up to the front of the boardinghouse and pulled open the door. Even from where he was standing, Red could see the filth sitting just inside the entrance to the place where Albright was staying. For a few cents a day other drunks and down-on-their-luck gamblers haunted the place like restless spirits.

Once Albright shut the door, Red stepped back into the fresh light of a new day. His eyes remained on the door for a few seconds, lingering there as he thought about the next move he planned to make. Now that the whore had done her job, the other man he'd hired had worn Albright down.

Actually, "hired" wasn't the correct word. All he'd had to do was drop Albright's name in the right company and provide the man's whereabouts to bait an eager young fighter into taking the job. Kids like that were easy enough to find. Red should know, since he'd once been one of them.

And now that Albright's nerves were thoroughly shredded, he was ripe for the picking, just as soon as Red decided to walk up and take what was his. By the look on Albright's face, death would be a blessing.

It was almost sad, Red thought. To see a man driven down so low that he didn't even value his own life anymore.

Then again, Red valued Albright's life enough for the both of them. The way he saw it, Albright was a big enough name that killing him would allow Red to raise the prices on all of his jobs to almost double what they'd once been. Business was like that. Kill one for free and kill the next twenty for double.

It was a smart investment.

The only thing that could possibly get in his way was the unexpected arrival of Clint Adams. Red knew that Albright and Adams had known each other, but he surely didn't think he'd see them both in the same place. Not that that would change his plans any. On the contrary, if Red played his cards right, he just might be able to take them both down before leaving Lumley.

After that . . . he could name his price for the rest of his life. He could make a killing.

Red chuckled to himself and headed back to his hotel.

TWENTY-SEVEN

Despite all that had been said and all the bad memories that had been dredged up, Clint felt good when he made it back to his hotel without passing out from fatigue along the way. He'd been in to check into his room and drop off his things when he'd first arrived, but that seemed as though it had been years ago. Now, walking through the door when a couple guests were just about to check out, Clint smiled at the very thought of dropping himself down onto the bed in his sparsely furnished room.

The place wasn't much to look at, but it had the essentials: a chair, washbasin, chest of drawers and a bed, complete with a thick, clean quilt. After taking off his boots and stripping off his shirt and pants, Clint climbed beneath the covers and . . .

. . . he didn't remember much of anything until he opened his eyes several hours later.

He awoke to a sound that Clint thought, at first, had only been in his head.

After talking about it all night, Clint had dreamed of the time he'd spent in Briar, Nebraska, and he thought he could still hear the sound of Jack's footsteps on the loose floorboards of the saloon where he'd called out Sean.

Then Clint swore he could hear gunshots, except they still seemed to be coming from far away. Once they were gone, he heard the sound of a body tapping against the floor after being shot.

. . . tapping . . .

. . . knocking . . .

Clint reluctantly peeled his eyes open. Taking a moment to reacquaint himself with his surroundings, he heard the sound again. It was definitely knocking.

Clint sat up in bed and reached down to pluck his shirt from where he'd tossed it onto the floor. "Come in," he croaked while slipping his arms through the sleeves.

The door handle rattled a bit, stopped, and then there was another knock.

Realizing he'd locked the door, Clint pulled some air into his lungs and climbed out of bed. "I'm coming," he grumbled. After rubbing some life back into his eyes, Clint pulled on his pants, unlocked the door and twisted the knob.

Outside, there was a small, narrow-boned woman who Clint didn't recognize right away. But just as she was starting to speak, Clint realized that she was the woman who worked at the front desk and had even been the one to check him in when he'd first arrived.

Clint did his best not to appear too cross as he said, "What can I do for you?"

Apparently, he didn't do a very good job, since the small woman still seemed to back away as though she was afraid that he might take a bite at her. "There's a visitor to see you," she said meekly.

Another deep breath was all Clint needed to soften his expression enough to put the woman at ease. "Really? Who is it?"

"It's Maggie Doyle." She said the name as if it was something that should have been familiar to him. And when she saw the perplexed look on Clint's face, she added, "From the sewing shop."

Rather than try to pull any more details from the mousy desk clerk, Clint simply nodded as though he had any clue as to what she was talking about. "Just let me straighten up and I'll be right down."

The woman nodded. "I'll have her wait in the dining room. If you like, I can fix you an early lunch."

"Actually, I was thinking about a late breakfast."

"We might be able to scrape something up. We had quite a showing this morning and there might not be a lot left."

"I'll take whatever you can offer. I'm sure it'll be wonderful."

Even though he hadn't put the slightest bit of flirtation in his voice, Clint noticed that the woman seemed to blush a little and turn her head down. A little smile appeared on her face and her eyes lingered on a spot just below Clint's neck.

When he looked down, Clint realized that his shirt wasn't quite buttoned all the way. On the off chance that it might give him a better shot at scoring a hearty breakfast, he left his shirt just the way it was.

"I'll do what I can."

"That's all I can ask," Clint said with a polite nod. "Now, if you'll excuse me . . ."

Suddenly, the woman seemed flustered, and she quickly turned on the balls of her feet to head down the hall toward the top of the stairs. "Of course, of course," she stammered. "I'll just run down and tell Maggie that you're on your way."

Before Clint could thank her, the clerk was gone. Her footsteps clattered on the floor like tapping broomstick handles. She took the stairs so quickly that Clint kept an ear open for the sound of her taking a fall. Once the steps faded away, he laughed softly to himself, stepped back inside his room and shut the door.

"What I won't do for a decent breakfast," he grumbled while pulling on the rest of his clothes and making sure everything was buttoned this time.

In less than five minutes, he was out the door and walking toward the stairs. Already, he could detect the scents of coffee brewing and bacon frying. It all smelled so good that it was easy to see why the hotel's restaurant did a good business every morning.

Since Clint hadn't even known the place had a restaurant when he first checked in, it took him a minute or two to find it once he was downstairs. His nose did most of the work, and he followed the delicious aromas to a small door at the end of a narrow hallway just past the front desk.

That door opened up to a fairly large dining room that was teeming with workers clearing away the breakfast dishes and straightening up the mess that the morning crowd had left behind. There were only a few tables occupied by customers and Clint scanned them, hoping that the woman who'd come to see him at least recognized his face.

Two of the occupied tables had couples sitting at them and Clint passed those over for the time being. Instead, he focused on the remaining three with one person each. Of those, one was a man in his late forties working on a thick cut of ham. Another was a redhead with an impressive body wrapped up tightly beneath several layers of shawls, scarves and a high-collared dress. At the last table, there sat a woman with her back to him and dark brown hair tied into a thick braid.

As he looked over all these people, Clint racked his brain for any memory connected to the name of Maggie Doyle. No matter how hard he thought about it, he simply couldn't come up with any recollection of the name or any face to associate with it.

He decided to own up to his ignorance and just start trying to find her the hard way.

Clint walked up to the closest table first, which had a man and woman sitting at it. "Excuse me," he said quietly. "Do you know a Maggie Doyle?"

"We're from Arkansas" was the stiff reply from the man.

After apologizing, Clint went to the redhead. "Maggie Doyle?"

Although the redhead looked happier to see him, she didn't respond to the name.

"I'm Maggie Doyle," came a voice from the next table.

Clint looked over to her, and suddenly he was taken back to that day ten years ago when he and Sean had saved that stagecoach from being robbed. The attractive brunette had looked at him just as warmly then as she did right now.

TWENTY-EIGHT

Clint's mind swam with all the memories he'd been reliving ever since he'd come back to meet with Sean. Everything from the first fight with Mike all the way to the battle at the stagecoach had been coursing through Clint's brain in a constant stream.

Until now, he'd been focusing mainly on what he and Sean had been doing at those times. Now, as he looked at the brunette's pretty face and wide, expressive eyes, Clint tried to recall as much as he could about what had happened to her at those times ten years ago.

For the life of him, he couldn't recollect much of anything about her.

Clint shook himself out of his thoughts and pulled out a chair at Maggie's table. "Sorry," he said, "but I didn't recognize your name when I heard it from the woman who came to fetch me."

Her voice was smooth and deep, yet utterly feminine. "There's a good reason for that."

"I just woke up, and I've been having a hard time ever since I got into town the other day."

"That, and you've never heard my name before in your life until today."

Nodding, Clint tried not to look half as foolish as he felt. "You know, I think I like that explanation better. It makes me look a little less ignorant."

They both laughed at that before Maggie reached across the table. "It should be me that apologizes since I kind of snuck up on you without much warning. I'm Maggie Doyle."

"Clint Adams," he said, taking her hand and shaking it gently. "Pleased to meet you."

Maggie wore a simple, yet elegant dress that was the color of coffee with the slightest touch of cream. It hung on the edge of her shoulders, with a neckline that swooped just low enough to display the upper curve of her large, round breasts. Her skin was a dark golden color that looked more Spanish than Mexican and seemed to blend in nicely with the hue of her dress. Smiling with full, soft lips, she took her hand back and turned her face down slightly.

"Now that we've been properly introduced, I don't feel so bad," she said.

Clint couldn't help but stare into those large, chocolate brown eyes. "You shouldn't feel bad at all. This breakfast promises to be one of the best I've had in a long time."

"Maybe you should wait until you hear about why I've come to see you."

Before she could explain any further, Maggie had to wait while one of the waiters came by to take their order. First of all, Clint was informed that breakfast hours had been extended and that he could get anything he wanted. After passing on his gratitude to the desk clerk, Clint ordered steak, eggs and coffee. Maggie stuck to lunch.

"Does everyone wake up and eat at the crack of dawn around here?" Clint asked once the waiter had left.

"We're a lot of farmers in this town. Either that, or we grew up on a farm. One way or another, it tends to make you an early riser."

"So what brings you here? Do you live in Lumley?"

Maggie nodded. "My family moved here from Briar after . . . all the trouble that was going on there."

That brought the memories flooding back through Clint's mind one more time. "Seems like you're not the only one. Sean Albright's here also."

An unpleasant look drifted over Maggie's features at the mention of Sean's name. Clint was certain he saw a trace of disgust in her eyes.

"I know he's here," she said. "Everybody knows that."

"Is he why you came to see me?" When he asked that, Clint noticed that Maggie seemed even more uncomfortable all of a sudden. "Not that I'm complaining, mind you. I just got the impression you had something important to talk to me about."

Their drinks were set in front of them and Maggie waited until the waiter had gone before continuing. "Actually, he's only part of the reason I wanted to see you." Maggie looked up at Clint as if she was waiting for something. Once she knew she had his attention, she went on. "Are you here because of what happened?" The question seemed to take all the courage that she could muster just to speak out loud.

Now Clint was more interested than ever. "Actually, no. I just came by to see what Sean was up to. It seems that he's been up to something, but he doesn't really want to tell me about it. That and it's been . . . hard for him to talk to me."

After a single blink of her eyes, Maggie cut through all the padding Clint had been trying to put on his explanation. "You mean because he's been drunk?"

"Yes . . . that's pretty much what I mean."

"Well, he spends a whole lot of time drunk. It's been that way for several years now."

"That would explain why I haven't heard from him for so long. Do you still keep in touch with him?"

Maggie shook her head as though the very idea was absurd in her mind. "My family and I moved here because we knew he'd settled down here. We thought he could protect us especially after all he did in Briar." Now it was her turn to take a moment and pore over her memories. "After you left, we got ourselves a new sheriff and Briar prospered like you wouldn't believe. Even after Sean left, the whole town seemed to be . . . I don't know . . . cured somehow."

"Cured of what?"

Maggie's cheeks flushed a bit and the corners of her mouth turned up in a pleasant little smile. "It must sound odd to a man like you, but we felt as though the town had been cleaned out of a bad element."

"If I remember correctly, your old sheriff was a pretty bad element."

"Yes, but the peace didn't last too long. After a while, we got bigger and gunfighters started bringing their shooting and killing to our town again, but Sean had moved on. Eventually . . . so did we. I tried finding you, but we only caught up with Sean. He was a familiar face and someone we thought we could rely on."

"And were you right?"

"No, Mr. Adams. It was the worst mistake we could have possibly made."

TWENTY-NINE

This time, Clint wasn't at all surprised by what she'd said. In fact, he would have been more surprised if he'd heard Maggie say something nice about Sean Albright. "And why is that?" he asked, hoping to finally get an explanation.

"Mr. Albright is nothing but a drunk and reckless man. It was pure luck that we found him as we traveled through Kansas, but it was obviously bad luck."

Rather than rush the young woman, Clint let her take her time and speak at her own pace. After a long pause, she stared down at her hands, which were clasped in front of her on top of the table, and let out a slow breath.

"That man brings nothing but trouble," she said with a trace of pity in her voice. "He's always getting into fights and someone always winds up dead. Sometimes . . . the dead people aren't even the ones who had anything to do with him."

"What do you mean?"

"I've seen him get into more shootouts than I ever thought possible. Frankly, I'm amazed he's not dead yet since he's drunk most of the time. Some of the stories I heard say he once shot four men when he was only after two . . . because he was seeing double. I've seen him kill one man after trying to run away into a crowded saloon. Three men died that day and all they were doing was standing at the bar."

Shaking his head, Clint pointed out, "You can't blame Sean for that. Nobody can."

"Three weeks ago, a man rode into town saying that he wanted to kill Mr. Albright."

"A gunfighter?"

Maggie nodded. "He said his name was Red Maddox and he waited around at every saloon, talking to anyone who would listen about how he was going to challenge him to a fight that would prove Mr. Albright wasn't so tough after all. Everyone in town thought there was going to be another gunfight and everyone waited to see how Mr. Albright would react. He didn't show his face for three days. That's when this Maddox fellow started getting impatient. He said that he would start killing a man every day that Mr. Albright didn't come around. He called it practice."

Hearing this, Clint started to feel a cold, angry knot forming in the pit of his stomach. He also had a pretty good idea of where this story was headed.

Maggie went on, her voice starting to waver slightly as she remembered the details of her story. "That was two weeks ago, Mr. Adams. And Maddox has been true to his word."

"Good Lord," Clint said in a low voice. "How come I haven't heard about this until now?"

"Because folks around town are good at recognizing another gunfighter when he comes here. Ever since Mr. Albright decided to stay in Lumley, there have always been gunfighters coming around looking for him. That's just the way it's been . . . even before me or my family got here."

Clint took this in, thinking about everything that Sean

had told him the night before. Hearing things from this perspective, Sean's words made a lot more sense. Up until this moment, Clint had been starting to think his old friend was simply paranoid after a life that had been lived too fast. Now it seemed that although Sean was obviously a wreck, he at least wasn't crazy.

Another thing that seemed a little strange was the fact that Clint couldn't recall introducing himself to more than one or two people in Lumley. If they'd recognized him, they surely hid it well, since nobody called him by name. "So everybody here knows who I am?"

"Of course," Maggie said with a beaming smile. "Everybody knows The Gunsmith."

At that moment, the waiter came back with a full plate in each hand. Clint felt as though the last two words that Maggie had said were still hanging in the air over the table for all the world to see. Much to his dismay, the waiter did seem to look at Clint with a strange look in his eye even after the food had been delivered.

"See," Maggie said. "Even he knows."

THIRTY

Freezing with his fork poised halfway between the plate and his mouth, Clint looked up at Maggie just as she raised her hand to cover the smile she wore. "All right," Clint said after setting down the bit of steak he'd cut, "you people have an eye for faces, I'll give you that much. That still doesn't explain why some men I'd never seen before in my life tried to shoot me the other day."

"What?"

Clint took a few minutes to tell Maggie about the men who'd shot at him when he first came close to town limits. Between bites, he also explained a little about what had happened between him and Sean the night before.

"It's no wonder," she said when Clint was finished. "Those men you saw just lost a brother to Maddox the day before you arrived. If you mentioned Mr. Albright . . . especially being who you are . . . they might have thought you wanted to start even more trouble in town than there already was."

"Trouble? If they know who I am, they should know I don't start trouble wherever I go."

The look on Maggie's face was akin to that of a schoolmarm who'd just caught one of her pupils in a lie. She

stared down her nose for a few seconds and raised her
eyebrows so that Clint could almost picture wire-rimmed
spectacles perched on the end of her face.

"What's that look for?" he asked.

"Think about what you said for a moment and then try
to think about how others see you."

Clint did as she asked while slicing off another piece
of his steak. And the more he considered his life and all
the extraordinary events that filled it, the more he could
see how easy it would be to get a different impression.

Sure, he always tried to help people whenever he could,
and that required him to use his gun from time to time.
When he thought about how others would see the same
instances, he realized how unnerving it would all seem,
to have a gunfight roll through a normally peaceful town,
leaving broken windows and bloody bodies in its wake.
No matter what the results were, such a thing would still
be awful strange for the people who were used to living
their quiet, boring lives without incident.

"You know something?" Clint said. "I never thought
about it like that before."

Shrugging as she took another bite of the sandwich
she'd ordered, Maggie said, "Well, don't feel too bad. I
know those men you were talking about. They probably
didn't mean to kill you. I'm sure they would've much
rather liked to put a bullet or two into Mr. Albright's
hide."

Finally, Clint was getting a better picture of what was
going on in Lumley. He was a ways off from seeing the
entire picture, but at least a few pieces were falling into
place. "So you never told me why you came to find me.
I'm guessing it wasn't just to get a free lunch."

Maggie's face became serious once again and she fidgeted in her chair for a few seconds before answering. "No.
It wasn't just for lunch, although I've wanted to meet you
for an awfully long time."

Clint's mind drifted back to that day ten years ago. Even with a decade sitting between now and then, he could still see Maggie's eyes taking him in and watching every move he'd made. The effect of those eyes upon him hadn't lessened one bit over the years.

Although it was an effort for her, Maggie eventually got the strength to speak again. When she did, she looked around first and then leaned in closer. "There's going to be more trouble," she said in a whisper. "Some of the men in town aim to get together and take Mr. Albright to Red Maddox. They figure that'll end the killings and bring Lumley back to the way it was."

Clint thought about the time he'd spent with Sean and the emptiness that seemed to have taken over the other man's spirit. No matter how bizarre the locals' plan might be, Clint knew there was a chance that if they did come for him, Sean might very well let them have him.

"When did you hear about this?" Clint asked.

"Just this morning. Some of the town law were getting together to decide what they should do about all of this."

"The town law? Why would they consider something like that when they could just arrest Maddox?" Suddenly, Clint's eyes flashed with anger. "In fact, why haven't they done anything about this?"

"Because Maddox is too much for them. They were going to ask Mr. Albright to leave town, but . . . they know who he is and what he's done. They think he might kill them just like he killed that sheriff in Briar."

Clint pushed away from the table and got to his feet so quickly that he almost sent his chair toppling to the floor behind him. "This is too much," he said, just barely keeping his voice down. "Where's the sheriff's office?"

Reaching out to take hold of his arm, Maggie stood up and looked him square in the eyes. "You don't have to do any of that," she said soothingly. "I talked to him the moment I heard. It didn't take much to talk them out of such an insane idea, but something still needs to be done about Maddox. That's why I came to you."

The rage that had flared up in Clint's system burned through his blood until he was finally able to cool off. "At least someone around here is thinking straight. I still think I should talk to the local law, just to get a better idea of what we can do."

"What do you mean?" Maggie asked. "You know what to do. You need to find him and kill him, that's all."

Clint looked deeply into Maggie's eyes. He didn't see any doubt or fear inside of her. On the contrary, he saw complete confidence in what she'd proposed. More than that, as Clint looked around the dining room, he saw the same hopeful look in every one of the faces turned toward him.

Taking Maggie by the hand, he turned and walked toward the front door.

"Clint, where are you going?" she asked.

"Out of here."

"Why? What's wrong?"

"I'm starting to think that Sean might just be the sanest man in this whole place."

THIRTY-ONE

As Clint led Maggie from the hotel, one notion flew through his mind after another. First, he wanted to get over to the sheriff's office and see just what the hell the town's lawman could be thinking in letting such a strange notion get so close to happening. Then, he thought about what Maggie had said and how easy it had been to stop it. And that was where his thoughts hit a snag.

It sounded as though it had been easy for her to stop the plan to deliver Sean to his death. Much too easy.

When he'd taken himself and Maggie out of the hotel and across the street, Clint stopped and let go of her arm.

All the while, she'd been asking him questions and trying to catch his attention. But only now did her words register in Clint's mind.

"What's the matter?" she asked. "Where are you taking me? What's going on?"

"I want to talk to him," Clint stated.

"Talk to who?"

"Maddox. I want you to tell me where I can find him so I can talk to him for myself."

"Are you going to fight him?" she asked with that same, hopeful wide-eyed expression. "I knew you would. Even when I saw you ten years ago, I knew that you would never walk away from someone who needed you. You'd never let anyone get away with—"

Clint interrupted her with a quick wave of his hand and a sharp tone. "That's enough, Maggie. Whatever you or anyone else thinks about me or Sean, I don't want to hear about it anymore. I don't even want to hear about what the sheriff has to say. The only person who can straighten things out for me is Maddox. If he's really here in town, then take me to him."

"What do you mean *if* he's here? Don't you believe me?"

"I've heard so many stories lately that I don't know what to believe. All I'm sure of is that if Maddox isn't here, then I can't talk to him and the problem is gone. If he is here, I'll have to see him for myself sooner or later, so it might as well be sooner, before anyone else gets hurt."

Maggie pressed herself a little closer against him, her eyes locking onto Clint's. When she spoke, the heat from her breath brushed over Clint's skin like a warm breeze. "I knew you'd help us, Clint. The moment I saw you again, I knew you could help us better than anyone else."

Although Clint couldn't deny the attraction he felt for her, he also couldn't overlook the fact that she seemed to be more than attracted to him. The way she looked at him still reminded him of that girl from ten years ago who watched him like he was some kind of larger-than-life figure straight from the pages of a yellowback novel.

Maggie turned away just then, as though she sensed what Clint might be thinking. "I know I must sound like a little girl to you. It's just that, ever since I saw you that day, I always knew that you were the one who'd brought about the change in Mr. Albright. If you hadn't been there . . . Lord only knows how he might have turned out."

"I've thought about that a lot, myself. Sometimes I

think things might have turned out much better if I hadn't been there at all."

She looked at him then as though Clint had said something blasphemous. "Don't even talk like that. I might not have know him too well, but Mr. Albright wasn't headed for a very bright future. He even rode with that crooked sheriff of ours for a bit. A blind man could see that he was about to join up with him until you showed up and made him look before he took that road."

Clint regarded her for a few seconds and then slowly shook his head. "You know an awful lot about Sean for someone who says they didn't know him very well."

"It's not anything that anyone in Briar couldn't see as long as they had their eyes open."

"Well, you'd be surprised how many folks all over the world seem perfectly happy living with their eyes closed."

A moment passed between them where each person got a quick glimpse at what the other was truly made of. When Clint looked at Maggie, he saw not only a beautiful woman, but someone who had a firm handle on the way things worked around her. The image of her as a wide-eyed little girl was fading fast, leaving him with the picture of her here and now. Ten years had left their mark on her body as well as her mind. She was a woman now, and no stranger to the cold, hard facts of life among the wolves.

He could tell that she was changing the way she thought about him, as well. The hero worship was gone from her eyes. Instead, she looked at him as someone she could talk to. Someone she could trust . . . at least for the moment, anyway.

"If you want to see Maddox, I'll take you to where he normally spends most of his time," she said. "It's not too far from here."

•　•　•

As soon as they arrived at the Charleston Saloon, Maggie stopped and pointed to it with an offhanded wave. "This is it," she said. "If he's not in there now, he'll be along soon."

Clint examined the place quickly, noting that it seemed to be one of the nicer saloons he'd seen in a while. Although it wasn't too big, every window was clean and every board was well maintained. Even the handle and hinges on the front door looked as though they'd recently been polished. In fact, Clint knew that if he'd had more time to look around Lumley for himself, he might have chosen to spend some time in the Charleston, as well.

Maggie gave him a quick description of what Red Maddox looked like and then leaned in to give him a quick kiss on the cheek.

"What was that for?" Clint asked, unable to hide his surprise about the kiss.

"Luck." Her cheeks blushed slightly and a little grin came onto her face. "And I've wanted to do that for ten years. I'll wait out here for you."

"You'd better not. I don't know this man too well and if things get rough, I don't want you anywhere you might get hurt."

"But I—"

Clint silenced her by placing his fingertip gently upon her mouth. Just then, he felt the connection between himself and Maggie intensify like a sudden crackle in a campfire. Before he knew it, he was leaning forward to kiss her again, only this time it was longer and deeper, leaving them both wanting more.

When they pulled away, Maggie was the one wearing the surprised look on her face. She quickly blinked it away and her smile grew larger. "Should I even ask what that was for?"

"Let's just say that I've also regretted some missed opportunities."

She nodded and took a few steps back. As she moved away, she kept her eyes on him, as though she didn't want to let him out of her sight. Finally, she spun around and walked quickly away, forcing herself to keep from looking back.

As much as he liked watching the way she moved, Clint forced himself to look away from Maggie. That memory of her as a wide-eyed girl was fading farther and farther away with every passing second.

THIRTY-TWO

The sunlight penetrated the flimsy curtains on the single window in Sean Albright's room. It invaded his space and burned his eyelids like the uninvited visitor it was. As always, his head was pounding with the remnants of all the alcohol-induced nightmares that had tortured him the night before. He was left with a blinding headache and the sickening knowledge that he now had to confront yet another day.

It was all still there. Every one of the memories, every bit of regret, all the demons floating around inside his mind were all still right where he'd left them before the first drop of whiskey had passed his lips. And along with all of that, there was something else. There was that extra bit of knowledge that he also had to deal with Clint Adams, on top of everything else.

Sean tossed off his dirty sheets and swung his legs over the side of his rented bed. The room stank of stale liquor along with traces of opium. His clothes lay crumpled in a pile next to the bed and his gun lay on the opposite side of the room. After rubbing his eyes for a few minutes, he stared at his gun belt as though it was a ghost that had come to haunt him. Every part of his soul wanted to open the window and toss that pistol out, never to see it again. But he might as well try to do the same to one of his arms or legs.

The .45 was part of him. That much was certain. It had been a part of him since he'd taken his first life. Ever since that day, he'd only needed it more and more, to fend off those that came to take his life from him.

That was the part that always made him laugh. Even though he knew his life was a festering pile of trash, he simply couldn't just throw it away. Perhaps something deep down inside of him wanted to live.

Then again . . . there could just be another part of him that was afraid to let go. Just as he was afraid to go on.

His head was starting to hurt even more just thinking about it. And rather than entertain those thoughts any more, he got up, pulled his clothes on and opened the door. Perhaps some breakfast would help him feel better. He might even run into Clint again along the way.

No matter how much Adams preached to him, Sean still wanted to see the man now that he was sober enough to have a real conversation. Taking a deep breath, he stepped into the dirty hall of his boardinghouse and started to close the door behind him.

He couldn't do it, though. Sean struggled to keep walking, but he just couldn't take another step.

It was a struggle he went through every day. Every goddamn day, and it never changed. If he tried to fight it, the headache only got worse, soon to be followed by a twisting in his gut and a queasiness in his soul. With everything that was going on, Sean knew he had to try and straighten himself out, if only to look better in Clint's eyes.

Grudgingly, Sean gave in to the compunction that kept him from leaving his room just yet. He reached through the door to grab hold of his gun belt and then strapped it around his waist. The weapon felt good hanging from its usual spot. The weight of it was a constant reassurance that every piece of him was present and accounted for.

Sean decided to try and keep his chin high and go about his life. After shutting the door, he took off down the hall and eventually stepped outside. It was a clear day and the wind was blowing just enough to cool his skin. Folks seemed happy enough as they walked by, but Sean knew better than to try and start up any conversations or even make his presence known.

They all knew he was there. They just weren't happy about it.

Sean put them out of his mind, as well, and continued along his way.

The walk actually did him some good. He'd taken the long way around town, which added an extra half hour to his trip. Right about then, his stomach was starting to growl with hunger and the alcohol was almost burned from his system. His steps were steady, but the headache and nausea hung in as a reminder of the past night's indiscretions.

Figuring that Clint would want to eat at the hotel he'd stayed at, Sean eventually made his way there. Normally, he stayed away from that particular restaurant because it was usually so crowded. But this time, he was willing to put up with the looks he'd get from the locals. After all, it had been a good long while since he'd had a truly good meal.

Sean was thinking about what he might order when he spotted someone staring at him out of the corner of his eye. Usually, he made a point not to notice every person that stared at him, but his instincts forced him to turn to look at this one. It didn't take long to see why.

The man was no more than twenty-two or twenty-three. Sean had seen him around town a few times, mainly around the saloons and cathouses. After straining through his brain for a second or two, Sean was able to come up with the young man's name.

"Good mornin' to you," Sean said in the friendliest voice he could manage. "Tom, is it?"

The youth nodded sharply. "Yeah, that's right. Tom Jensen."

Sean kept walking. "Just out for something to eat, so I'll let you get on with your business." And with that, he turned his back on the other man and quickened his pace.

"That's right," Tom called to Sean's back. "You'd best run if you know what's good for you."

Those words stung Sean, but he choked on them and kept walking.

"I'm callin' you out," Tom shouted.

Stopping, Sean took a deep breath and turned back to face the younger man. "Why would you want to do that?" he asked in a voice that naturally took on a deadly edge. "You'd only get yourself killed and what would that prove?"

"It'd prove that I'm twice the man you ever was. And it would also make me a rich man. Mr. Maddox is offering five hundred dollars for your head and I'm the man to collect it."

Sean had had more than enough practice to know that Tom would not allow himself to be frightened off. Even though the youth's nerves were on edge and his hands made tense fists as he talked, Sean knew there would be no diverting him.

Taking a few steps toward the youth, Sean fixed his eyes on the kid and thought back to the days when he'd been that eager to throw himself in front of a bullet. He knew all to well what it was like to be so certain in the speed of your gun arm and the strength of your soul. He knew exactly how the kid felt at that exact moment: invincible.

Sean only wished he could feel a fraction of that inside of him anymore.

In the few moments that had passed in silence, Tom had started to fidget back and forth from one foot to another. His eyes twitched and fluttered open and shut, betraying the nervous energy building up inside of him. To Sean, all of these things were like writing on the wall. Every twitch was a warning, just as each quick breath signaled what was about to come.

Before the kid's fuse could burn all the way down, Sean said, "If you're in such a hurry to get to your grave, then that's your problem. I'll send you there once I get something in my belly."

"No! We'll do this right—"

"You'll have your fight, boy. Meet me back here in an hour. At least let a man have his breakfast in peace. Or are you worried you'll lose your nerve by then?"

Sean knew damn well that the last question would be enough to do the trick.

"Fine," Tom said. "One hour. That's all you got . . . or . . . or I'll come looking for you."

"I'm sure you will, kid," Sean grumbled as he started walking back toward the restaurant. "I'm sure you will."

THIRTY-THREE

Clint was just about to walk into the Charleston Saloon when the front door opened and a tall figure stepped out onto the porch. The moment Clint saw him, he knew this was the man he'd been looking for. It wasn't so much that he recognized the man's face, but he recognized something about the way he carried himself. There was a certain confidence in the way he moved that connected with Clint on an almost primal level.

They looked at each other for one second, and it was plain to see that the man was sizing Clint up in much the same way.

One man of the gun to another.

"Red Maddox?" Clint asked.

The man leaned slightly on his silver-tipped cane, tipped his hat and nodded curtly. "Right you are, sir. And I suppose that would make you Clint Adams."

Clint nodded as well.

"I've been told you were in town," Maddox continued. "And we have met before, although I doubt you would remember." Red's Louisiana accent made it sound as though his tongue was wrapping around every syllable, slowly tasting it before letting it slide from his mouth.

"I don't recall."

Red waved his hand dismissively as though he was swatting at an annoying insect. "It was some time ago in New Orleans. I was just a face in the crowd then, watching you handle a rough bunch who didn't appreciate losing their money to you over cards."

Despite everything he'd heard about the man, Clint's first reaction was to like him. But then he focused on the killer instinct lurking inside of the man's eyes. That part of him was well hidden, but could be spotted easily enough by someone who knew what they were looking for. Once he saw it, Clint felt as though he'd spotted a shark swimming just below the surface of an otherwise calm pool.

"I'll take your word for it," Clint replied. "Do you mind if I speak to you for a moment?"

"Of course not. In fact, I was just about to find you."

There was a steely edge to Red's statement. Although subtle, it implied quite a bit. First there was the calm indifference to the weight carried by Clint's name. Also, there was the impression that Maddox had been circling Clint long enough to strike whenever he desired. He wasn't about to *look* for him. He was about to *find* him.

"Well then, since we both have things on our minds, I'll just start this off quickly," Clint said. "I've been hearing some rumors around town that you have a problem with a friend of mine."

"I have a problem?" Maddox asked, his voice dripping with sarcasm. "I suppose you're talking about Mr. Sean Albright?"

"I am."

"Why, I assure you, the only problem I have with him is finding him. Once I do, the matter between him and myself will be concluded."

"And why do you want to find him so badly?"

"In his years of drunken bar fights and cowardly attacks

on well-meaning persons of my acquaintance, he's managed to kill several very good friends of mine. I believe the names Charlie Bowders and Sam Stockwell are familiar to you?"

Clint recognized those names, but only barely. They were both fairly well-known gunslingers in the southeast. They'd gotten their reputation more for the number of men they'd killed than for taking part in any events of real importance. "I've heard of them. If I remember correctly, neither one of them was good for much of anything besides holding up banks and hiring out his gun to whoever could cough up five dollars."

If Maddox was affected by Clint's words, he did a good job of hiding it. Instead, he smiled without humor and tapped his cane on the boards beneath his feet. "That's no way to get on my good side."

"Actually, that wasn't a big concern of mine. All I came to ask was how you've been going about trying to find Sean Albright."

"And why would that concern you, the high and mighty Gunsmith, himself?"

"It doesn't. Sean can handle himself well enough." Taking a step closer, Clint continued, while watching Maddox very carefully. "The part I didn't much care for was when I heard that you'd taken to killing innocent people just to draw him out."

Maddox's face gave nothing away. His features might just as well have been carved in stone, since they didn't shift in the slightest. When he spoke, his eyes remained fixed on target like drills that had already started twisting into Clint's skull. "I spoke to your friend when I first arrived. This could all have been over that day, but he decided to run and hide from me like the cowardly soul he is."

"Is what I heard true or not?"

"I'm here for a purpose, Mr. Adams. You, of all people, should appreciate that."

Clint's face had become impassive as well. His muscles tensed beneath his skin, giving his entire body the look of carved granite. "Answer my question."

Without the slightest bit of guilt or remorse, Maddox replied, "it is."

"Then I'll have to ask you to stop."

Maddox dropped his stony facade by turning his head ever so slightly and grinning. "I've heard plenty of things about you, Adams. I know a lot about what you do and how you act, but I also know you're not the law. You can't make me do anything."

"I said I was asking you to stop. That's all."

Maddox didn't make a move toward his gun. He didn't have to. Every part of his body shifted slightly and his entire bearing reflected that he was ready to fight. His eyes became calm and cold. His head lowered just a little bit, the motion resembling that of a serpent preparing to strike. "And if I refuse?"

"Then I'll have to kill you."

THIRTY-FOUR

Clint could tell what Maddox was thinking just as well as if the other man had been screaming it into his ear. Both of them were no more than six feet away from each other, but the tension between them connected them to each other like a bond of blood.

The look in Maddox's eyes had gone from easy confidence to a silent warning, and finally settled on direct challenge. Clint could tell that the Southern man wasn't used to being spoken to with such bluntness. In fact, that seemed to be the only thing to throw Maddox off his game. As much as Maddox wanted to draw his gun, and Clint could feel that he wanted to *very* much, he wasn't about to do it. Not just yet, anyway.

That showed Clint another part of Maddox's personality. Not only was he supremely confident in himself, but he was smart as well. That made him a dangerous man.

"I'm not after you, Adams," Maddox said in a strained, yet controlled voice. "If I was, you'd know it."

"Then why were you out to find me just now?"

"To tell you exactly what I did. I've got no fight with you. I know Mr. Albright is a friend of yours, but there's no reason for his misfortune to affect you as well. Once my business with him is over, I can deal with you if that's the way you'd like to play it."

"So you're just making sure that you get one of us at a time," Clint said. "Trying to make sure you don't have anything stacked against you. Am I getting close here?"

"Yes. Very close indeed."

"Well, maybe you should have thought about that before you started shooting folks that don't want a part of any of this."

"The law doesn't care about that," Maddox said with a sneer. "As long as Albright gets taken care of, they figure it's worth any price that needs to be paid."

"Somehow I doubt that. In any case, the law isn't your problem at the moment. I am."

Maddox's features intensified even further. The look on his face was one of aggression that was just barely being kept at bay. He was itching to pull his gun, but something inside of him prevented him from following through. Suddenly, his eyes darted to a point to Clint's left and Maddox gripped his cane even tighter. "Well, now. Speak of the devil."

Although Clint could hear footsteps approaching him from behind, he knew better than to turn around for a better look. Whoever it was must have sensed this and stopped walking almost immediately.

"It's me, Clint," Sean said. "What's going on here?"

Taking a step back, Maddox kicked open the Charleston's door and raised his free hand in the air. His other remained fixed to his cane, but he held it now with a fraction of the grip he'd exerted only moments before. "Since I'm not one for gatherings, I'll take my leave . . . for the moment. Sean, you know where to find me. I suggest you hurry."

And before another word could be said, Maddox turned on the balls of his feet and stepped inside the saloon. The door swung shut with a gentle tap.

Clint had seen enough of the man to know better than to follow Maddox inside. Instead, he turned to face Sean, noticing immediately how different the other man looked.

"You got some rest, I see," Clint pointed out. "It suits you much better than the way I found you."

Sean's eyes were bloodshot and rimmed with dark circles. His skin looked pasty and loose on his bones. "Yeah . . . I feel better."

It didn't take a doctor to know that Sean must have been hurting after the hell his body had been through. Even Clint could see the stoop in his posture and the pained way he squinted, as though blinking would have caused more agony than he could bear.

Sean looked up at the front door of the Charleston and then glanced quickly from side to side. "Let's get going," he said. "I was hoping to get some breakfast before—"

"What's the matter, Sean?"

Blinking nervously, Sean took another look at the street on either side and then back to the saloon. "What? Why do you ask? Nothing's wrong."

Clint studied him for a moment or two, watching the way he fidgeted on his feet like a nervous child. The other night, Clint figured that Sean's odd behavior was caused by all the alcohol he'd poured down his throat, but this time the man didn't reek of whiskey and he didn't stagger when he walked. There was a different stench about him that pored from the center of his very being. And it was something that Clint never would have thought he'd sense coming from this man.

Rather than say anything right away, Clint tested his theory by staying put and ignoring Sean's obvious attempts to get him to leave.

Before too long, Sean started to get more anxious. His eyes checked the same three directions again and again while his thumbs pulled nervously at his gun belt. "Are we going to go, or would you rather stand here all day?"

"What's your hurry?" Clint asked. "Doesn't it bother you having someone kill folks for no good reason? Or is that just another one of those stories you were telling me about?"

"No . . . that's no story. I just . . . It's just that . . ."

"Hey, Albright!"

The voice came from farther down the street and when Clint turned to look, all he saw was the spindly form of a youth carrying a gun that looked as though it weighed more than him. At first, Clint couldn't believe that this boy had been the one to do the shouting. But that surprise was nothing compared to what he saw when he turned back to look at Sean.

Sean was still looking at the figure in the distance when he caught Clint's gaze. He then straightened up and gave him a thin, unconvincing smile. "Just some loudmouthed kid," he said. "How about that breakfast?"

As if in response to what Sean had said, Tom took another step forward. "What's the matter? You need help to take me on? If that's the case, I'll shoot both of you down right here and right now."

Clint was in no mood to be threatened by a scrap of a man like this. "Mind your manners, kid. You don't want any part of either one of us."

"It's not you I want," Tom said while slapping the palm of his hand against the handle of his gun. "It's just Albright. I'll take you later if you want. None of you gunfighters scare me."

"Jesus," Clint muttered. "Sean, who the hell is this?"

But when Clint turned, he stopped himself short. Sean was nowhere to be seen.

THIRTY-FIVE

As Clint stood there looking for Sean, he almost forgot about the kid who'd called his name. In fact, he'd started to walk away and search for any trace as to where Sean had gone, when he heard Tom's voice ringing through the air.

"I knew he was too yellow to fight me," the kid said. Turning to face Clint with an air of even greater cockiness, he asked, "Why'd he come to you? Probably to get you to help him take me on, I'll wager. He must've heard about those men I killed outside of Topeka."

Clint turned to face the kid as he became more and more annoyed with the entire situation. "Look, I don't know who the hell you are and I don't know about any men in Topeka."

"Well, there was four of 'em and—"

"And I'm sure it was a sight to see and all of that, but I still don't know you. So why don't you do us both a favor and just go off and tell someone about it who gives a damn."

Even from where he was standing, Clint could see the angered expression on the kid's face. Tom bristled and shifted on his feet, his hands opening and closing as though he wasn't quite sure what he should do.

"I know who you are, Mr. Adams," Tom said. "And when I'm done with your yellow friend, I'll be back for you. When you catch up to him, tell him I'll be waiting to finish this."

It was all Clint could do to keep from laughing in the boy's face. He thought back to the times when he'd seen Sean in action and knew that his friend would never have turned his back on a small-timer like this. "Take my advice, kid, and be grateful that you didn't have to do this. I can tell you right now that Sean would have killed you where you stand."

"Yeah," Tom said with a snide grin. "Too bad he ran away before he could prove that to me himself."

With no trace of Sean to be seen, Clint didn't have much of an answer for that. So rather than swap threats with the kid, which he wasn't accustomed to doing anyway, Clint turned away and walked in one of the few directions that Sean could have gone without being seen. A quick glance over his shoulder told him that Tom had also headed off in another direction, no doubt to spread the news of his "victory" to anyone who would listen.

The street was a straight shot all the way through town, bordered on both sides by storefronts with alleys between them. As Clint walked, he glanced to either side, looking for any sign of Sean or where he might have gone. He was almost at the end of the block when he spotted his friend at the entrance to a general store.

Clint stopped and looked at Sean, waiting for an explanation.

Strangely enough, Sean appeared as though he didn't have a care in the world. His face was alight with a broad smile, and when he saw Clint, he held his arms out wide as if he hadn't seen him for several years.

"Clint, my good friend. I hope the people you've met today haven't given you the wrong idea of Lumley. In fact, this place is a rather nice town to live in."

"What the hell is going on?" Clint asked after stepping up onto the boardwalk next to Sean. "Do you mind telling me just what happened back there?"

For a second, Sean tried to look confused, but he dropped the charade quickly enough. His face then twisted into a scowl as he waved dismissively toward the distant Charleston. "Oh, forget them. I don't see the reason in catering to a bunch like that. You get those types in every town and you can't fight them all, right?"

"No, but you also need to know when you have to face someone like that out of necessity. And that kid . . . do you know what he was talking about?"

Shaking his head, Sean said, "I walked away when Maddox was spewing his threats. I'll get to him soon enough."

"So you didn't see that kid? And you didn't hear him screaming out your name?" Clint asked suspiciously.

"Like I told you the other night, there's always some-one calling me out. It never ends. I've learned to block it out most the time, or else kids like Tom wouldn't even let me get a decent meal without asking for a shot at me."

"Then you did see him . . . Otherwise you wouldn't know his name."

Sean flinched as he tried to think of something else to say. His mouth hung open as he searched for the right words, but then he finally shrugged in his familiar way and took another tack. "All right, so I did see him, but I've got better things to do right now. Especially with you in town. I thought we might catch up on old times before you had to head out again."

For one of the few times in his life, Clint was genuinely unsure as to what he should do next. What he knew about Sean and the way he handled himself was flying in the face of what he saw right now. The man he'd known was confident and ready to take on any obstacles set before him, either with or without resorting to violence. But the man who stood before him was nothing like that. He was a nervous, fidgeting, shifty man who blatantly lied to his friends and ran away from the simplest challenge that any man of the gun could face.

Kids like Tom were more common than a brown cow and they could be turned away with little or no effort. To run away from someone like that was more than a shot to a man's pride. It was proof that he no longer had any.

Clint followed Sean down the street, electing not to ask him right away about why he felt the sudden need to shop when he had someone ready to draw down on him. They wound up at a small restaurant that was mostly full with locals enjoying an early lunch. As soon as most of them got a look at who'd just walked in, however, the place began to empty out.

By the looks of him, Sean didn't seem to notice. But Clint noticed well enough for both of them. In fact, he was beginning to see why Sean was getting this reaction on a daily basis from the people around him.

THIRTY-SIX

The restaurant's owner seemed more than a little reluctant, but he eventually came over to serve Clint and Sean. Normally, Clint might have thought to ask why he was getting such obviously bad treatment, but the more time he spent in Lumley, the more he began to expect such a reception.

Besides having a cold spot in their collective hearts for Sean, the locals didn't have much use for anyone who wore his gun as though he knew how to use it. It was as though they saw every such person as an outlaw or killer. Strangely enough, that didn't seem to put much of a dent in the town's gunfighter population.

Rather than try to make any sense of it, Clint decided to do what he could for his friend and then leave town for greener pastures as soon as possible. More than anything, he would have liked to pick up and go right then and there, but he simply couldn't let Sean remain the way he was. His friend reminded Clint of a wounded animal, limping about as best he could, not altogether sure as to what was ailing him.

While they drank the water that had been brought out to them, Clint listened as Sean prattled on about a whole lot of nothing. He seemed to be filling the air with words

just so he wouldn't give Clint a chance to say what needed
to be said. And rather than interrupt, Clint listened patiently, waiting for the right opportunity to broach the real
subject.

Just as Sean was about to launch himself into another
story from the past, the restaurant's door flew open, slamming against the wall hard enough to rattle the front window. Clint turned in his chair and saw a boy no more than
ten years old charge into the room, panting for breath.

"Scotty, what's wrong, lad?" the restaurant owner
asked as he ran from around the counter.

Wearing a ragged jacket that seemed to weigh more
than his entire torso, Scotty pulled in a few gasping
breaths and pointed wildly out the door. "It's . . . it's Mr.
Maddox! He says . . . he's gonna kill another one if . . ."

At that moment, Scotty's eyes fell upon Clint's table.
The rest of his sentence snagged in his throat when he
saw Sean sitting there.

The owner glanced back with a distasteful look and
turned his back on both men. "It's all right, son. Just say
your piece."

Standing on tiptoe to look over the crouching man's
shoulder, Scotty gazed at Sean one more time before
whispering, "He says Mr. Albright needs to come see him
or he'll shoot another one."

"Who is it, son? Who will he shoot?"

"Maggie Doyle."

Hearing that name, Clint shot to his feet, sending his
chair rattling to the floor behind him. He stepped toward
the owner and asked, "Where is he?"

The young boy pulled back reflexively, but he couldn't
go far since the owner had ahold of both his shoulders.
He seemed frightened, but still managed to look up and
lock eyes with Clint. "The Charleston," he squeaked.

Clint made an effort to soften his tone. Since the owner
made it clear that he would protect the boy as much as

he could, Clint didn't try to get any closer. "How did you find out about this?"

"Clint . . . we can't do anything for her," Sean said from the table. "If I just leave town, then maybe Maddox will just—"

"Will just what?" Clint said over his shoulder. "Will he just give up and leave everyone be? Or will he just kill her before that and follow you to the next town to start the same thing again?"

Sean pleaded with his eyes as he looked around nervously. "Come on. Just let me take off and you can handle this if you want. I thought you didn't even believe that Maddox was doing any killing anyway."

"Well, there's one way to find out for sure." Turning back to the child, Clint said, "Go on. Tell me the rest."

After receiving a nod from the owner, Scotty swallowed hard and said, "I was going by the Charleston when Mr. Maddox stepped out. He had Miss Doyle and told me to spread the word and if I . . . if I found Mr. Albright to pass him a message."

Sensing the child's reluctance to go on, Clint hunkered down to his level and said, "It's all right. Nobody's going to be mad at you. Just say what he told you. Mr. Albright's listening."

The child squirmed for a few seconds as though his skin was suddenly too tight and then he rubbed his nose. "He said that if Mr. Albright was a man at all, he would face him . . . or else whatever happens to Miss Doyle is on his head."

Clint straightened up again and didn't even bother looking over his shoulder when he said, "I don't know about you, Sean, but I think someone should go and see what Maddox wants." Now he did turn. When he did, he was almost surprised to find that Sean hadn't run out again. "If you won't go, then I will."

Drawing in a deep breath that somewhat resembled the

ones Scotty had taken, Sean placed his hands on the table and pushed his chair back from it. He then rose to his feet as his hand drifted down to rest upon the handle of his gun. Nodding more to himself than anyone else, he said, "Fine. Let's go."

The restaurant owner picked Scotty up off his feet and carried him to the back of the room, where he sat him down on top of the counter. He tightened his grip on the boy instinctively when Sean walked over to him and tossed some money down next to him.

"Here," he said. "Take this and keep the change." Looking past the man and winking to the child, he added, "You've got a fine boy there. Tell him to keep away from saloons. Nothing good comes out of them."

With that, he turned and stepped toward the front door. Clint looked Sean over carefully, examining the man to make sure he wasn't about to buckle under the pressure which still ravaged his eyes and caused sweat to form in a thick layer on his brow.

"You ready?" Clint asked.

"Yeah," Sean replied, despite the much different story told by the look in his eyes. "Let's get this over with."

THIRTY-SEVEN

Clint led the way out the door with Sean right behind him. At that moment, he was reminded of the day ten years ago when they'd both set out to take on another threat. The difference between those two instances was like night and day, and so was the difference in the man at Clint's side.

Once they were outside, Sean's steps became slower, until he eventually came to a stop. Suddenly, his breath was coming in ragged gasps and he bent at the waist like an old man trying to pull in his last lungful of air.

"I can't . . . do this, Clint. There's no need. Maddox is bluffing. He'll let her go. We don't have to—"

Clint could feel the heat welling up in his body as he spun around to face Sean. "I've had just about all I can stomach of this," he said without even trying to hide his anger. "You've never run away from a fight as long as I've known you. We might have lost contact over the years, but when we did get together, you proved yourself to be as solid as a rock."

He tried to hold his tongue, but Sean had begun to crack. His shoulders slumped forward and his hand shot to the inside of his jacket to remove a brass flask. With

149

trembling fingers, he removed the top of the flask and poured its contents down his throat. When he pulled it away, whiskey drizzled from its lip as well as from the corner of his mouth.

"Maybe I was never the man you thought I was," Sean said, his voice cracking after the passage of the whiskey. "I tried to tell you before, but you just wouldn't listen."

"I've listened for the last two days," Clint snapped. "And all I've heard was a lot of drunken bellyaching. Everyone has problems, Sean. You could've done a lot of good . . . you *have* done a lot of good and now you just let yourself fall apart. Over what? Some people out to prove themselves against you? That can't be all! You're stronger than that."

"What am I supposed to do?" Sean asked. "You want to hear me say it? You want to break me down all the way? I'll say it then." He took a quick pull from the flask and wiped his mouth with the back of his hand. "I'm scared. You happy? I've been scared for years, and no matter how much I try to build a new life, I can't get away from my old one. You may be fine with living by the gun, but I'm not! You did a lot for me, Clint, and I really appreciate it, but I can't live like you. I thought I was a man of the gun, but I'm not. It may be in my blood, but the only thing that does is make it harder for me to quit."

"You can't ruin your whole life," Clint said. "It's not even worth it to try such a thing. Whatever your lot is, you've got to face up to it if you want to change it. And now that other people's lives are in the balance . . ."

"I know, I know. Maddox is only one man. If I leave, then he won't have any choice but to move on."

"Maybe. But I can't take that chance. Not when there's even the slightest possibility that someone else might die because of it." Clint saw the way Sean was shrinking away from him, even when all they were doing was talking. As much as he hated to admit it, Clint knew that Sean would only be a liability if Maddox decided to push their meeting into a fight. Finally, he let go of his memories and faced up to what had to be done. "I'll take care of this. Just promise me one thing."

"Anything, Clint."

"When you get a chance, let me know where you've gone. And try to stay away from the whiskey. I hate to think of you like you were the other night."

Nodding, Sean took a long look at the flask in his hand and tossed it into a ditch. "You got it."

Clint turned his back on the other man and started once again walking down the street toward the Charleston. Already, he could see a crowd gathering in front of the saloon. A glimmer shone from the middle of the crowd as a beam of sunlight glanced from the silver top of a polished cane. Using that as his focal point, Clint set off.

Sean's voice came from behind him, somewhat weaker than it had ever sounded before. "You don't have to do this, Clint. This is their own problem. Their law chose to look the other way. You don't have to make up for that mistake."

"Somebody has to," Clint replied. "Might as well be me."

This time, Clint started walking and decided not to stop no matter what Sean chose to say. No more words came from the man on the street behind him. And although it was a hard thing to do at that point in time, Clint put Sean out of his mind. There were bigger things to handle right now.

THIRTY-EIGHT

By the time Clint made it to the front of the Charleston Saloon, all of the dozens of locals gathered around it had their eyes trained on him. Ignoring the looks from the others, Clint set his gaze on the only one there he was after. And like a man hosting a formal gala rather than one picking a fight, Red Maddox stood at the center of them all leaning regally upon his cane.

"Are you here to watch your friend die?" Maddox asked, his Louisiana drawl making every word drip like honey. "You weren't invited, but you're more than welcome to bear witness."

"Where's Maggie?" Clint asked. His voice cut through the air like a bolt of steel.

With a flourish, Maddox motioned toward the front of the saloon where two men held Maggie Doyle between them. One of the captors was the young man who'd called out for Sean minutes before. Although Tom didn't look like he was enjoying himself, the young man seemed more than ready to do whatever Maddox asked of him.

Maddox looked at Maggie and then back at Clint, seeming to be very proud of himself as he said, "Mr. Albright may not be the most forthcoming of men, but he does leave quite a mark wherever he goes. Drawing him out has been a particularly . . . messy affair. I hoped that today would be the end of it."

"If it's a fight you want," Clint said, "you can bring it to me."

Only the most expert of poker players would have recognized the slip in Maddox's facade upon hearing that. Clint knew how to read men like newspapers, and to him, the flinch was plain as the nose on his face.

But Maddox kept his front up well enough . . . at least well enough to convince himself, anyway. "I'm not after you. I believe I told you that before."

"You sure did. And I've got no quarrel with you. So why don't you just forget about hurting anyone else, hand over the woman, and we can all go about our business? Then if you want to face Sean, you can do it man to man."

The two holding Maggie were becoming anxious. They looked at each other and then to Maddox, hoping to get an order so they could do something about the nervous energy coursing through their bodies. Maggie stood between them without putting up much of a fight. Instead, she looked at Clint without the slightest bit of doubt in her eyes that he would come through for her.

Maddox locked eyes with Clint for a few seconds before looking toward the crowd. He then scanned them, searching for something that he never seemed to find. "Unless you heard me incorrectly, sir, my original offer still stands. I'll let the woman go when I see Mr. Albright in front of me. Make me wait too long, and she dies . . . right here, for all to see."

Clint's features hardened as he quickly took stock of the layout. In the blink of an eye, he calculated angles and judged what each of the three men might do. When he was done with that, he turned to those who'd gathered around and shouted, "All of you can go home! Get away from here before anyone gets hurt."

Like a flock of startled sheep, they all stood rooted to their spots, unsure of whether or not they were going to move. All doubt inside of them vanished, however, when one of the men holding Maggie took the matter into his own hands.

Tom shoved Maggie roughly to the ground, his eyes burning with his single-minded purpose. "I've heard enough of this talk! If you're scared to take on Clint Adams, then step aside and leave him to me."

Without looking back, Maddox smiled broadly and stood his ground even as the locals around him bolted in every direction like a stampede.

Although Clint was surprised that the younger man made his move first, his instincts wouldn't allow for him to be caught off guard. He didn't move a muscle until he saw that Maggie was in the clear. By then, Tom had grabbed for his gun and was in the process of pulling it free from its holster.

The only reason Clint waited another fraction of a second was so he could see what the other two men were going to do. It seemed that Maddox was content to remain where he was for the moment, but the other young man next to Tom had a desperate look in his eyes and would surely follow his partner's lead.

Clint's hand flashed toward the Colt, plucked it from his side and brought it up in a single fluid motion. Tom was still thumbing back his hammer when Clint squeezed the trigger and the Colt barked once amid a plume of smoke.

The single piece of lead hissed through the air like a viper, boring a trail straight toward Tom's chest and thumping through the young man's flesh on impact. When it punched through the other side, it dragged Tom with it as though he'd been tied to the back of a runaway horse. He was lifted back a step and came down roughly on his flailing boot, wobbling there like a drunk as blood streamed down the front and back of his shirt.

Rather than shoot the young man again, Clint turned his attention to the one who'd been holding Maggie's other arm. That one had managed to clear leather with an old Army-issue pistol and was bringing it up so he could sight down its barrel.

"Don't," Clint shouted.

The other youth either didn't hear the warning or chose to ignore it. Either way, he fanned back the pistol's hammer with his left palm and took a quick shot.

From where he stood Clint could see the kid's hand shaking, and an instant before the gun went off, he dropped to one knee and fired his Colt. The first shot grazed the youth's shoulder, spinning him in a tight semicircle. But that wasn't enough to keep him from fanning back the hammer again while pulling the gun back on target.

Cursing to himself when he saw the youth refusing to pull back, Clint fired almost simultaneously with the kid. Their guns roared together, filling the air with a fiery thunder that tore through Clint's ears like claws through bared skin. He could hear the bullet whip past his head, no more than an inch or two away from his temple. But Clint didn't waver in the slightest as he fired again through the smoke that had settled like a veil between the two men.

For a moment, the second youth merely stood in his place, staring angrily at Clint. Then, his eyes rolled back into his head and blood started to flow from the third eye just beneath his hairline. Letting his arms drop to either side, the young man dropped to his knees and then flopped over to one side.

Now Clint turned his attention back to Maddox. He stared at the well-dressed man down the barrel of his gun. "Maggie," he said without taking his eyes away from his target. "Are you all right?"

She stood up and shakily got to her feet. As she

climbed down from the saloon's front steps, she almost fell to the ground, as if her legs were too unstable to carry her. Unable to get out more than a stifled syllable or two, she raised her hand in a quick wave as she jogged away from the Charleston.

Satisfied that she was at least well enough to move, Clint said to Maddox, "You still want that fight, or have you seen enough?"

"Those were just eager gunhands," Maddox drawled. "There's plenty more where they came from."

Clint eased the Colt back into its holster and gave Maddox a look that was filled with the promise of death. "This ends here and now. If I hear about you threatening one more innocent, whether it's here or any other town, I'll kill you where you stand. Do you understand me?"

After a tense pause, Maddox nodded with an almost unnatural calmness. "You can tell your yellow friend he's still on my list. And I'll have you know . . . so are you."

With that, Maddox turned and walked up to the Charleston, making sure to step over the bodies as he went inside.

THIRTY-NINE

Clint didn't bother sticking around to see how the crowd would react to his battle with Maddox's men. All he saw as he turned to walk away was the surprised looks on all those faces. Some of the people started to smile once they saw the show was over, and they all began whispering excitedly to the people next to them.

The only thing Clint was looking for was a sign that Maggie was all right. He'd seen her move away from her captors right before the shooting started, but after that he'd been a little too preoccupied to keep track of where she'd gone.

Glancing toward one of the biggest clumps of people, Clint saw her separate herself from the rest and come running over to him.

"I knew you'd come for me," she said breathlessly. "I just knew it."

Clint looked her over carefully. "Did you get hurt?"

"No. A little shaken up, but nothing permanent. It was worth it to see you again. It was so . . . exciting."

"Yeah, well, I aim to please." Clint turned away from the whole mess and started to walk away. He wasn't ex-

actly sure where he was headed. He just knew that he
wanted to get away from the Charleston.

Rushing up to his side, Maggie took hold of his arm
and spoke in an excited chatter. "What about Mr. Maddox?"

"What about him?"

"Well, he's still . . . alive."

"You say that like it's a bad thing."

Maggie paused for a second, obviously giving a little
more thought to what she should say. "It's just that . . . he
said he'd still be coming for you and Mr. Albright.
Doesn't that worry you?"

"No," Clint said. "It's just something I have to learn to
live with. I can't spend every waking hour fussing about
it. When Maddox screws up his courage again, he'll make
his play. I can tell you for sure that he won't be dragging
anyone else into it again."

"How can you tell for sure?"

Thinking back to the last exchange he'd had with Maddox, Clint thought about the look in the other man's eyes.
Everything from the way his voice had come out to the
way he squared his shoulders told something to those who
knew what to look for. "Trust me. Maddox may talk
tough, but he knows if he'd come close to drawing his
gun that he would have been dead before his finger
touched the trigger. He'll come at me or Sean again, but
it'll be a different way. That much I do know for sure."

Just then, Maggie stepped around Clint so that she was
directly in front of him. She reached out to place both
hands on his chest, stopping him in his tracks. "Clint. I
want to show you something."

Before he could say anything in protest, Maggie lifted
a finger and placed it against his lips. "Please. Just come
with me."

She took his hand and led him down another street for
a couple of blocks. As they walked, the mood between

them started to lighten up a bit. Rather than talk about
Sean or gun battles or anything to do with the things that
had been absorbing Clint's life for the past few days, they
talked like old friends catching up on the years they'd
been apart from one another.

Even though Clint hadn't even known her name when
he'd first seen her, he still felt a vague connection to Maggie, which had been established by nothing more than a
powerful look that passed between them ten years ago.
From that starting point, they talked about what they'd
been doing in that time and where they'd gone. Clint only
touched on a couple of his travels, but Maggie was more
than willing to share all she could about her life. And
surprisingly enough, Clint was happy to listen to her.

She spoke with a joy in her voice about what a cher-
ished life she'd led. To most people it would have
sounded common, but her happiness was strong enough
to infect them both.

"It's all because of you, Clint," she said after stopping
in front of a small, well-kept building in the middle of
Lumley's shopping district.

Clint looked puzzled for a second. "What's all because
of me?"

Smiling warmly, she opened the door to the store. A
sign hanging near the front window read, "Maggie's Sewing Circle." The inside was filled with threads of all colors, sewing needles, thimbles, even finished products,
ranging from quilts to linens to curtains.

Once inside, Maggie held her arms out to either side
and spun around in a wide circle. "Everything . . . all of
this . . . I owe to you," she said.

Glancing around at all the various doodads, Clint ap-
preciated the nice little shop, but was still waiting for her
words to make some sense. "I guess I still don't understand."

She moved back to him and wrapped her arms around

him. "I would have been dead ten years ago on that stage if you hadn't showed up to save my life and the lives of those other passengers. We would have all been dead if it wasn't for you."

"And Sean," Clint added. "It was his show. I was just there for the ride."

"But he wouldn't have been there without you. I've thanked him already, but I remember that day like it was yesterday. You killed the man who was about to shoot every one of us in that stage. I thought I was going to die and you kept me alive. And ever since that day, all the things I've done and every thing I've seen is because you made it possible."

She leaned in closer then, pressing her body against his and brushing her lips against his neck. "Thank you," she whispered. Both words made a puff of air on Clint's skin that sent chills down his spine.

Clint did his best to keep himself collected, even as Maggie rubbed her body slowly against his.

"I don't expect anything from you," he said. "For what I did, I mean. You don't have to do anything to repay me if . . ."

Smiling, Maggie ran her fingertips down Clint's chest, slipping them between the buttons whenever she could. "That's not what this is about. This is about what we've been feeling ever since that first time we looked at each other ten years ago. And ever since that time, I've been expecting something from *you*."

Clint took hold of her and grasped her tightly. "What have you been expecting?" he whispered into her ear.

"For you to make love to me."

FORTY

Hearing those words was all Clint needed to push him over the edge. Maggie's voice was so insistent and so warm against his skin that he felt a sudden need to touch her body and feel his hands pressed against her bare skin. When he brushed his palms over her shoulders, Clint restrained himself from tearing off her dress the way he'd been wanting to. Instead, he lightly grazed her shoulders and traced a gentle line where her clothing met her body.

Maggie sighed deeply and closed her eyes, leaning her head back to fully enjoy the sensation that she'd been dreaming about for so very long. His touch was a teasing flicker as it darted from the base of her neck, down the front of her chest, and even further, until his fingertips barely skimmed the upper slope of her breasts.

She arched her back and leaned against a post, rubbing one leg against Clint's thigh while tugging the bottom of his shirt from where it had been tucked into his pants. Once she could slip her hands beneath his clothes, Maggie used them to search his body, exploring every muscle and caressing every inch of him she could get her hands on.

Still stroking her upper body, Clint leaned in and touched his lips against her neck. He kissed her gently at first and then worked his way over her shoulder, nibbling at her skin as he went. She responded by groaning softly, her hands moving faster over his body in response to the feel of his lips.

Clint hooked his fingers beneath the edge of her dress, tugging it down past her shoulders until he could cup one of her large breasts. The material of her dress strained almost to the breaking point, but refused to tear, which only drove both of them to greater heights of anticipation.

Suddenly, Maggie lifted Clint's hand away and took a step back. Her eyes were smoldering with passion and remained locked on him as she moved toward the front door and hung the "closed" sign in the window. Once that was done, she unfastened her dress and let it fall to her waist as she slowly walked up to him.

Her body was full and round in all the right places. There wasn't the slightest amount of modesty in her eyes as she shrugged out of her dress and let it fall to the floor. In fact, when she saw his eyes moving over her body, she smiled as though she was basking in his attention.

Reaching out to put his hands on her, Clint watched as her dark nipples grew hard even before their skin made contact. He kept himself from touching her right away, prolonging the wait just to see how she would react.

"Oh, I can't wait," she moaned while taking hold of his shirt and tearing it open. "I've been thinking about having you inside me for ten years . . . Don't make me wait another second."

Now, Clint allowed himself to indulge in what he'd been thinking about and picked Maggie off her feet to set her down on a table covered with folded quilts. She landed with a naughty laugh, still working to pull the clothes off his body.

Once his shirt hit the floor, she all but ripped his jeans off. Her eager hands wrapped around his stiff penis and held him for a moment, stroking gently.

Clint's heart was pounding inside his chest. The feel of her hands on him was like a long drink of water after a day spent in the desert sun. When he opened his eyes, he found her staring intently at him, her full, soft lips curled in a delicious grin.

Almost instinctively, Clint leaned in to taste those lips, and she met him with a kiss so passionate that it lasted for several minutes before their lips broke away from one another. Clint's hands were probing her body as well, sliding between her legs, which she parted for him, to allow his fingers to slip inside.

As he gently traced along the lips of her vagina, Clint listened to Maggie's breathing speed up. Her hands stroked him faster while she started to squirm on the tabletop. She leaned her head back and slowly ran her tongue over her top lip as Clint began rubbing slow, small circles around her clitoris.

Slowly moving away from her, Clint took hold of both of Maggie's wrists and pinned them to the table on either side of her body. She looked at him with wild excitement at being restrained, her chest heaving in anticipation of what he was going to do next. Clint leaned in for a quick kiss and let their tongues dance around each other until he once again moved away.

He continued kissing her. First on the neck, then down her body and then between her breasts. When he ran his tongue along her cleavage, Clint heard a long, luxurious moan come from Maggie as she leaned back and pressed herself against his mouth.

Clint's tongue flicked over her nipples, moving from one to the other as he cupped her in the palms of his hands. She seemed unable to move as he took her nipple in his mouth and gently rolled it between his teeth. Just when she started to squirm, he'd lick the sensitive nub of flesh while caressing her body in his strong grasp.

Before too long, she moved her hands through his hair,

urging his head down between her legs. Finally, Clint allowed himself to be guided, and he watched as she scooted to the edge of the table and spread her legs open as wide as she could for him.

Her vagina was moist and warm against his lips. When he flicked his tongue out to taste her, she let out a loud moan. Maggie's entire body shuddered at his slightest touch, while her fingers ran through his hair.

"Oh, god," she whispered. "That feels so good."

Clint moved his face in slow, even motions. Up and down. Side to side. Lingering in places that made her cry out the most, until her legs closed tightly around the back of his shoulders. Clint's tongue was all the way inside her now. Maggie pumped her hips against his face, and when she felt him gently suck on her clitoris, she let out a cry of pleasure that echoed loudly through the entire store.

Getting back to his feet, Clint savored the taste of her which still lingered in his mouth. The moment he stood up, he leaned in and kissed her. Maggie responded instantly, kissing him with enough passion to make his knees buckle.

Her hands were on him again. They moved up and down his sides before wrapping around his cock and stroking him until he was so hard he ached to be inside her. Feeling this, Maggie smiled at him and fit him between her legs, shifting her hips until he could bury himself all the way inside of her, bringing a moan of ecstasy from both of them.

For a moment, Clint stayed still so he could savor the feeling of being completely enveloped by her body. Maggie's arms were locked around his neck and her legs were crossed behind his back. Her mouth closed around his tongue and her pussy closed tightly around the base of his cock.

When he moved his hips back, Clint felt the lips of her sex sliding along his shaft. The sensation was almost more than he could bear, and when he slid out of her, Clint saw Maggie look at him with renewed longing.

He pushed into her again, this time thrusting in and out with a quick pumping rhythm. She groaned every time he penetrated her, and Clint held on to her hips so he could pound into her a little harder. Soon, Maggie was lying with her back on the table, grabbing her breasts with both hands and squeezing her nipples while Clint thrust between her legs.

After a few minutes, Clint let her go and stepped back. When she opened her eyes, he was offering his hand to help her off the table.

"Please, Clint," she said with a little pout. "Don't stop."

Clint took hold of her, set her on her feet and turned her around. Coming up behind her, he slid his hands around to hold her breasts and whispered, "Don't worry. I'm not through with you yet."

FORTY-ONE

The solitary woman stood across the street from the sewing shop, watching the storefront while nursing her broken wrist. Lara had done plenty of things for money, but this was one of the hardest to do. Ever since the moment she'd agreed to work for Red Maddox, she'd regretted the decision with every bone in her body.

She wasn't a stupid woman. Lara had been around long enough and seen enough bad things to know what the world had in store for stupid people. But Maddox had dangled enough money in front of her to make her second-guess her instincts. And that, she knew, was her biggest mistake.

Normally, Maddox never asked her to do anything besides keep a man busy while he moved in for the kill. They'd done it several times and she'd always found it exciting. But once they'd started their operation in Lumley, things had taken a turn that she would never have expected.

When Lara was with Sean Albright, she'd actually started to care for him. But Maddox was still out to kill him. And though she knew that, she hadn't done a thing about it when the killer had come to pound in her door.

That notion hurt her even more than the shattered wrist Maddox had given her that same night.

Not even two days had passed since then, but Lara felt as though it was a lifetime ago. So much had changed in that time, mostly within her. She'd come to realize that, no matter how much she tried to justify what she'd done, she was still just a whore.

Whores did whatever they needed to do for money, selling themselves at any turn possible since that was the one thing that would always fetch a good price. She'd sold her body to men and then she'd sold her soul to Maddox. And since there was nowhere else to run from that cold fact, she figured she might as well see it through to the end.

"I've got one more job for you" was the last thing Maddox had said that night when he'd broken her wrist.

And this was it.

She was to keep an eye on Maggie Doyle because she'd been asking about Albright since she'd moved into town. Maddox was set to do anything and everything necessary to bring Albright into the open, and he knew that eventually Maggie would want to see him.

Lara told him he was wrong when she'd followed Maggie long enough to see that it was Clint Adams she was truly after. But that didn't satisfy Maddox. Not in the least. Instead, he'd set his sights on Adams, as well, giving Lara yet another thing to add to her long list of regrets.

She knew that she was helping get another man killed. She'd done it before, but that had been when Maddox had gunned for other killers. Lara knew who Albright and Adams were. They were gunmen, but they were also heroes. They'd saved plenty of people plenty of times and they did not deserve to die.

Pulling in a deep breath, Lara looked across the street at Maggie's sewing shop and wondered if she could truly go through with what she'd been planning. There was a time when she prided herself on being an independent woman full of pluck and confidence. Lately, Maddox had beaten that out of her, making her wonder if she really was half the woman she used to be.

Lara had seen the way Maggie looked at Clint Adams. She recognized that look because it was the same one she'd given to Sean not too long ago. She'd even given it to him that night when they'd made love. That night when she'd shown her true colors to the man who'd almost wound up dead in her bed.

Sean's words still stung in her mind. She remembered the things she'd said to him and the names she'd called him, but the truth was that she hated him because of what he made her realize about herself.

She truly was nothing but a whore.

No matter how many times she tried to justify what she did or how many ways she rearranged her thoughts on the matter, it always boiled down to the same thing. A whore sold herself to the highest bidder, which was exactly what Lara had done.

Her job was to fetch Maddox the moment she knew Clint Adams was in a vulnerable position. Maddox would then come and finish off Adams himself, since all of the men he'd hired to kill for him were already dead. It was a job Lara had done plenty of times, only this time there was a difference.

Good men would die this time. And they would die just to make a bad man look bigger.

It sounded too simplistic, but that was essentially what was going to happen. Life was truly simple, she'd found out a long time ago. The hard part was being able to face the essentials once they'd been laid bare in front of you.

It was even harder to get enough strength to change them.

FORTY-TWO

As Clint pressed his lips to the back of Maggie's neck and let his hands wrap around her body to caress her breasts, he didn't think about the eyes that might be watching through one of the store's windows. The curtains were mostly drawn, but there was enough glass exposed to let in the light, which flooded the shop with its warm glow. And the few times he did think about anyone walking by outside, the idea made what they were doing even more erotic. By the look in Maggie's eyes whenever she glanced toward the front door, she was thinking the same thing.

At the moment, however, the only thing Clint could think about was the softness of Maggie's plump buttocks as he pushed his hips against her. His penis grew harder by the second as it rubbed against her naked body. She reached behind to stroke its length while slowly wiggling her hips back and forth.

Clint's hands moved up the front of her body, touching either side of her face until he wrapped his fingers in her hair. Sensing what he wanted to do, Maggie pressed her backside against him and lifted herself up on her tiptoes. The moment Clint felt his cock slide into the moist slot between her legs, he pulled back on her hair and pushed himself in.

Maggie drew in a sharp breath when she felt him penetrate her body once again, and arched her back as he drove himself all the way inside. Clint's hips slapped against her round buttocks and he pushed as far in as he could go. Soon, he was pounding into her from behind and Maggie was leaning forward to grab the edges of the table.

Clint slid his hands down her back so he could hang on to her by the waist. Once she leaned completely forward, he was able to drive farther into her pussy, and he pounded inside of her until their bodies made a wet slapping sound as their skin met on impact.

Maggie's voice filled the shop, her wild groaning accompanied by the sound of their bodies coming together again and again. Finally, her sex clamped around Clint's member as a second orgasm started to work its way throughout her body.

The convulsions swept through her system, speeding her heart to an excited patter and forcing her to hold on to the table so hard that her knuckles turned a pale white. She could feel his hands holding her tightly, and when she turned around to look at Clint over her shoulder, she saw that he, too, was in the grip of ecstasy.

Clint buried his cock all the way inside of her moist folds, savoring the way her body took every inch of him while caressing him with her private muscles. She knew just how to press back against him and just when to wriggle her bottom to make every sensation feel as good as it possibly could.

Her plump bottom fit perfectly in his hands as he grabbed hold and thrust one more time to grind sensuously against her rounded curves. When he exploded inside of her, the pleasure was so great that he shouted out right along with her, their voices mixing to fill the empty shop with their cries.

Once his climax subsided, Clint pulled out of her and stepped back, allowing Maggie to turn around and take him in with her deep brown eyes. She gazed at him hungrily while her hands roamed over his body. She couldn't help but stroke his member with one hand while softly rubbing herself with the other.

"If I'd have known you were thinking of doing *that* for ten years," Clint said breathlessly, "I would have tracked you down a lot sooner."

Maggie cupped him in her hand while leaning forward to give Clint a deep, probing kiss. "You'd be surprised how much a girl can come up with after dreaming for that long. The more I heard about you over that time, the more I wanted to get you close to me again."

Clint picked up his clothes and was putting them back on when he spotted something through the front window. He couldn't see much because the curtains were covering most of the glass, but he did manage to get a glimpse of something that caught his eye.

"What is it?" Maggie asked when she saw him staring at something she couldn't quite see.

Clint was mostly dressed by the time he made it to the front of the shop. After hastily buckling his gun belt, he stood near the front door, with just a sliver of his body showing against the window, so he could peek through the glass without standing directly in front of it. "Somebody's coming."

Pulling on her dress, Maggie seemed too content to be concerned as she made her way to Clint's side and glanced through the window. "Oh, I wouldn't worry too much," she said. "It's only Lara."

"It's not her I was worried about."

"What do you—?" Maggie didn't have to finish her question. Because once she saw Red Maddox fall into step next to Lara, she started to get worried herself.

FORTY-THREE

"You did a fine job," Maddox said as he walked into the middle of the street next to Lara. "Of course, you've always done good work for me."

The gunman strode with his cane in hand as though he was out for a leisurely Sunday walk. His smile was anxious and victorious at the same time, and when he took in a deep breath to sample the air, he resembled a hunter surveying a room full of trophies.

Next to him, Lara couldn't have looked any more different. The shame in her eyes would have been obvious to anyone bothering to look for it. But she didn't bother hiding it because she knew that Maddox would not even think to look. Her thoughts still raced inside her mind, but she tried to keep the emotions from her voice when she asked, "Are you really going to take on Clint Adams by yourself?"

"Of course I am, darlin'. It wouldn't do to have it any other way." Squinting against the glare from the shop's front window, Maddox peered intently at the slim silhouette he could make out among the shadows inside. His eyes narrowed as he figured up his plan of attack while drumming his fingers upon the silver head of his cane. He knew better than to think that both Adams and Albright would run away scared. In fact, he'd been hoping that neither one of them would leave Lumley without allowing him to first pay his respects.

Maddox fought back the impulse to call Adams out like he was just some common target to be taken at his whim. He knew the stories about Adams were well founded and it was only a fool who'd go against such information as that. He did, however, get an idea as to how he could better approach the situation.

"Lara," he said to the woman next to him. "Be a dear and come here for a moment, will you?"

He waited patiently for a few seconds before spinning around with an angry glare in his eyes. Rather than find her waiting for him, Maddox could see no trace of the woman. Rather than waste time looking for her, he shrugged and turned back to the storefront. He'd gotten more than his money's worth out of that one anyway.

Noticing that the outlines he'd spotted moving inside the shop had gone, Maddox stepped lively and crossed the street. He headed for the sewing shop and then made a quick turn at the last second, nestling the walking stick beneath his arm as he went.

"Now where is he going?" Clint whispered to himself as he glanced out the window.

Maggie stood beside him, anxiously shifting from one foot to another while trying to look over his shoulder. "Who is it?" she asked.

"Maddox. He's decided to take the fight to me, I guess."

"What about Mr. Albright? He's been after him the entire time."

Clint shook his head and stepped away from the window. "Probably thinks I'm a bigger target," he said while pulling the curtain shut so that all of the window was covered. "Either that . . . or he couldn't find Sean."

In his mind, Clint figured that Sean was more than likely a long ways from town right about then. He didn't hold that against Sean in the least. He simply wished his friend all the best and hoped Sean would be in a little better shape the next time he saw him.

All those thoughts flew from his mind the moment he realized that he'd lost track of where Maddox had gone. Clint spun around and took hold of Maggie's wrist so he could lead her deeper into the shop.

"You should find somewhere to hide," he said. "If there's a back room or a storage closet or anything like that, I want you to get into it and don't come out until you hear from me. Understand?"

She was starting to look a little afraid, but nodded her head in the affirmative.

"Good."

She started heading for a small door at the back of the room, but stopped before disappearing inside the other room. Turning to glance over her shoulder, she asked, "Are you going to kill Maddox?"

"Only if he leaves me no other choice."

"Try to be careful. And remember that Mr. Albright needs you to do this for him."

And with that, Clint knew what all of Lumley really thought of Sean. The few that didn't hate his guts saw him as a pathetic shell of a man who could no longer defend himself without help. Clint might have felt sorry for him if he didn't think that Sean had been working long and hard on putting out that very image of himself.

"Just get someplace safe," Clint said. "And keep your head down if you hear any shooting."

Maggie ran back, kissed Clint quickly on the lips and then headed for the smaller room at the back of the shop.

Clint found his hat laying nearby and set it on his head, opening all of his senses for any trace of where Maddox would be coming from. Looking for any other ways out of the shop, Clint could find nothing else besides the front door and window. Left with no other choice, he opted for the direct route.

With his hand placed on top of his Colt and his reflexes coiled like a tightly wound spring, Clint threw open the front door and stepped outside. He immediately looked in the direction that Maddox had gone, but found nothing except for a lonely stretch of road and a deserted alley. Knowing better than to charge in blind, Clint moved across the street and started slowly walking down the boardwalk.

"All right, Maddox," he called out. "You wanted to see me . . . so here I am. Show yourself and say your piece."

For a moment, all Clint could hear was the restless wind blowing down the street and rattling nearby windows in their panes. He then caught sight of a quick glimmer of light coming from across the street and next to the front door of the building beside Maggie's shop.

Clint turned toward the glimmer, ready for anything. He found Red Maddox standing near that building, his gun already drawn and aimed at Clint's head.

FORTY-FOUR

"Good day to you, Mr. Adams," Maddox said cordially. "I must say that this is quite a surprise. Even after your little display earlier, I figured you for the type to let men fight their own battles."

"From what I hear, you've been doing your best to see that your battle involves everyone in this town."

Maddox shrugged. "The law don't seem to mind. Why should you?"

"I mind very much when someone starts shooting innocent people just to get their point across."

"None of those people had to die. If Mr. Albright had met me face-to-face when I first called him out, I wouldn't have had to resort to such drastic measures. Everyone in town realizes that. Why can't you?"

"Those people are scared," Clint said. "It's a whole lot easier for them to beat on someone who won't fight back than the man who's got a gun to their heads."

"Maybe so," Maddox said with a grin. "Or maybe your friend Mr. Albright is scared, as well."

Clint smiled right back at the man and shook his head. "You're not going to bait me, Maddox. If the law won't stand up to you, then I will. Either get out of town *right now,* or I'll throw you out. If you had any more men taking orders from you, I'm guessing you would've thrown them at me by now, so that means that you're all that's left."

"I'm plenty for you to worry about."

"Yeah, well, pardon me if I don't start shaking right away."

Finally, the smug look on Maddox's face dropped away, leaving the man's true nature behind. His features became stark and cold. His eyes glazed over like those of an animal that was about to have fresh blood coating its tongue.

"All right, Adams. I'm not about to leave this place until I have another kill marked up to my name. If you're so intent on being that kill, then I'll be happy to oblige you."

Clint didn't say a word in response. The time for talk had come and gone, leaving nothing but the present moment, the moment of truth, and an unknown stretch in between.

After stepping off the boardwalk and into the street, Maddox planted his feet in the packed dirt and shifted his cane from right hand to left. The sun was on its way down in the western sky, so its light fell down onto the front of Maddox's body and turned Clint's shadow into a long, dark wraith painted onto the street.

Once he was in position, Maddox slowly holstered his weapon and flexed his fingers over its handle.

Clint was surprised to see that gesture from his opponent. In fact, he was fully expecting to be ambushed long before he'd ever flush Maddox out into the open. Still, he wasn't about to be taken in just yet, and Clint's senses were still on alert for any trace of someone sneaking up on him from any direction.

Now that they were both there and waiting for the fatal second to come, neither one of them seemed in any hurry to rush their action. They showed no sign of restlessness or even eagerness to draw. They both knew it would come sooner or later. To champ at the bit now was the flaw of an amateur. Neither of them would be stupid enough to make that mistake.

Their eyes locked as though the twenty feet between them didn't even exist. Clint stood like a statue; the only part of him that so much as twitched was the heart thumping in his chest. Maddox gnashed his teeth, the muscles in his jaw pulsing with an erratic rhythm.

Finally, just as Maddox made a slight shift on his feet, Clint heard the sound of footsteps approaching quickly from somewhere behind him. His eyes darted in that direction for no more than a split second, but that was more than enough to set Maddox off like a sprung trap.

Clint spotted a twitch of movement in Maddox's gun hand. He saw the other man reach down for his pistol, which set all of Clint's reflexes into an instant response.

But rather than draw his pistol, Maddox lifted his other hand, which was wrapped around his cane. He shifted his upper body to the perfect angle to allow him to catch a bit of the sunlight pouring over him with the silver head of his cane. The dazzling rays bounced off polished metal and projected a spot onto Clint's chest, which Maddox deftly moved up into his target's eye.

Clint had already cleared leather and was about to pull his trigger when suddenly a blinding flash filled his line of sight and turned the scene in front of him into a haze of dancing lights and exploding dark blobs. Using his memory to guide his hand, Clint pointed the Colt toward where Maddox should have been and took his shot.

The gun went off once, but Clint could hear the shot whip through the air where it kept right on going.

Having mastered this maneuver years ago, Maddox was already on one knee and several feet to the side from where he'd been standing. Only now did he draw his gun and thumb back the hammer.

Although less than a couple of seconds had gone by, Clint knew that his time was quickly running out. He was able to blink away most of the glare, but by the time he could make out Maddox's form, another shot had already been fired, before Clint was able to focus his aim.

This shot found its mark and drilled into flesh. Gun smoke rolled over Clint's face and a pained grunt drifted on the breeze.

The footsteps behind Clint got closer, only now they were coming from a spot directly beside him.

Clint blinked once more, which was enough to clear most of his vision, except for a few stray blurs. His finger was clamped halfway down on the Colt's trigger, but when he got a good look at his target, he saw that Maddox was already laying on the ground with a gaping hole in his chest.

Turning to look toward the footsteps, Clint was ready to defend himself against whoever it was that had tried to sneak up on him. He didn't find any eager young gunfighter trying to make a name for himself, however. Instead, Clint saw a face that he'd almost forgotten.

"Sean?" he asked in disbelief. "What are you doing here?"

"Saving your ass, is what I'm doing," Sean replied in a voice that was strong and, more importantly, sober. He was the Sean Albright that Clint remembered and had almost given up for dead. There wasn't a trace of anxiety on Sean's face and not a hint of fear in his eyes.

FORTY-FIVE

Clint took a moment to make sure that Maggie was all right. She'd been hiding in the back room of her shop and burst through the door the moment she heard Clint call her name. Before she could say anything, her hands ran over his body and her eyes searched for any sign of injury.

"You're all right?" she asked.

Clint gave her a comforting hug and replied, "You sound so surprised. After the way you built me up over the years, I'd have thought you wouldn't expect anything else."

She smiled broadly and gave him a long, passionate kiss. "I heard the gunshots and feared the worst. I'm so glad you're not hurt. I always knew if anyone could handle Maddox it was—"

"Actually," Clint interrupted, "it wasn't me who handled him." In response to her puzzled stare, Clint led Maggie toward the front of the store, where Sean was waiting.

Outside, a crowd had already gathered around the spot where the undertaker was loading Maddox's body onto a narrow cart. Even from inside the store, the sounds of excited voices could be heard. Maggie looked at the scene for a moment before turning toward Sean.

"The sheriff's outside," Sean said. "Now that all the trouble's over, he finally decided to step in. He's looking for testimony and needs to talk to you, Miss Doyle."

Maggie nodded and started to walk out the door. She stopped at the last moment and placed her hands on Sean's cheeks. Looking up into his eyes, she said, "Thank you. For everything." Then she left the shop and headed for the clump of people in the street.

Once the door slammed shut, Clint walked up to Sean and held out his hand. It was immediately taken and both old friends shook as though they'd only just been reunited.

"I owe you a pretty big thank-you myself," Clint said.

Sean waved it off. "No need. After all you've done for me, I don't think we're even close to square."

"Did you follow Maddox when he came for me?"

"Actually . . . I was on my way out of town," Sean answered. The words hurt coming out, but it seemed to be a relief for him once they were in the open. "I was set to run. But someone came to stop me." Saying this, Sean glanced out the window and nodded.

Clint looked in the same direction and caught sight of Lara standing near the undertaker's wagon, lifting her splinted arm to return the greeting.

Sean shook his head and looked back to Clint. "That lady tried to kill me a few days ago and now she gives me the way to redeem myself. Guess I'll never figure out what the hell goes through a woman's mind."

"You'll never be alone with that problem."

"Differences or not, she came to get me just as I was leaving my boardinghouse. She told me what Maddox had planned and that he'd waited until this time of day so he could use that walking stick of his. Seems he's killed plenty of men with that little trick."

"I hate to admit it," Clint said. "But that move was

pretty impressive. He had the timing down well enough that it nearly put me out of my misery."

"Once I heard that, I ran here as fast as I could. I may be a coward, but I couldn't turn tail and walk away if I knew you might have to pay for my mistakes with your life."

"You're no coward, Sean," Clint said intently. "And I'll have words with anyone who says otherwise."

"Maybe, but I'm also not half the man I used to be. I thought I was a man of the gun, but that turned out to be a young man's pipe dream." Looking toward the floor, Sean let out a long, troubled sigh. "I just wish I could've learned that before I pulled my trigger that first time. I can still hear their voices, Clint. Every one of them men I killed . . . I can hear them like they was still begging for their lives."

"You'll learn to live with it," Clint said after a few silent moments passed them by.

"Guess I'll have to."

Clint slapped his friend on the shoulder as a way to break the somber mood that had descended upon them both. Sean lifted his head and smiled, looking more like his real self than ever.

"So where to next?" Clint asked.

"I think I'll hang up this chunk of metal for good," he said while patting the gun at his side. "It's done its part . . . and so have I. Maybe I'll buy myself a saloon somewhere where nobody's heard the stories about me. At least . . . not the bad ones."

With that, both men parted ways. Sean disappeared after talking to the town sheriff.

Clint moved on before anyone else who'd ridden with Maddox got any ideas in his head to pick up where his boss had left off. But even though Lumley was soon free of a gunfighter population, Clint knew the town would replenish its supply soon enough.

Another man of the gun would come to stake his claim in such fertile soil.

They would never stop coming.

Watch for

DEADLY GAME

249th novel in the exciting GUNSMITH series
from Jove

Coming in September!

J.R. ROBERTS
THE GUNSMITH

THE GUNSMITH #197:	APACHE RAID	0-515-12293-9
THE GUNSMITH #198:	THE LADY KILLERS	0-515-12303-X
THE GUNSMITH #199:	DENVER DESPERADOES	0-515-12341-2
THE GUNSMITH #200:	THE JAMES BOYS	0-515-12357-9
THE GUNSMITH #201:	THE GAMBLER	0-515-12373-0
THE GUNSMITH #202:	VIGILANTE JUSTICE	0-515-12393-5
THE GUNSMITH #203:	DEAD MAN'S BLUFF	0-515-12414-1
THE GUNSMITH #204:	WOMEN ON THE RUN	0-515-12438-9
THE GUNSMITH #205:	THE GAMBLER'S GIRL	0-515-12451-6
THE GUNSMITH #206:	LEGEND OF THE PIASA BIRD	0-515-12469-9
THE GUNSMITH #207:	KANSAS CITY KILLING	0-515-12486-9
THE GUNSMITH #208:	THE LAST BOUNTY	0-515-12512-1
THE GUNSMITH #209:	DEATH TIMES FIVE	0-515-12520-2
THE GUNSMITH #210:	MAXIMILIAN'S TREASURE	0-515-12534-2
THE GUNSMITH #211:	SON OF A GUNSMITH	0-515-12557-1
THE GUNSMITH #212:	FAMILY FEUD	0-515-12573-3
THE GUNSMITH #213:	STRANGLER'S VENDETTA	0-515-12615-2
THE GUNSMITH #214:	THE BORTON FAMILY GAME	0-515-12661-6
THE GUNSMITH #215:	SHOWDOWN AT DAYLIGHT	0-515-12688-8
THE GUNSMITH #216:	THE MAN FROM PECULIAR	0-515-12708-6
THE GUNSMITH #217:	AMBUSH AT BLACK ROCK	0-515-12735-3
THE GUNSMITH #218:	THE CLEVELAND CONNECTION	0-515-12756-6
THE GUNSMITH #219:	THE BROTHEL INSPECTOR	0-515-12771-X
THE GUNSMITH #220:	END OF THE TRAIL	0-515-12791-4
THE GUNSMITH #221:	DANGEROUS BREED	0-515-12809-0

Delivers more bang for the buck!

To Order call:
1-800-788-6262

(Ad # B111)

The New Action Western Series
From the creators of LONGARM!

DIAMONDBACK

Smooth as a snake—and twice as slippery—Dex Yancey is the con man's con man. Whether the game is cards, dice or gambling with your life, Dex is ready to play against the odds—and win. Ladies love him. Gamblers hate him. But *nobody* pulls one over on Dex....

❑ **DIAMONDBACK**   0-515-12568-7
Dex didn't much cotton to the family business—a cotton plantation—but he was still mighty riled when his brother, Lewis, cheated him out of his inheritance. So Dex decided it was time to show Lewis a thing or two about brotherly love.

❑ **DIAMONDBACK #2: Texas Two-Timing**   0-515-12685-3
While passing through Benson, Texas, Dex sees a chance to make some easy money. The local gentry challenge him to a horserace, and Dex—with a little ingenuity—comes in first place, naturally. But when he tries to collect his winnings, he's accused of cheating.

❑ **DIAMONDBACK #3: Raking in Revenge**   0-515-12753-1
When Dex and his friend James rode into Texas, they weren't looking for trouble. But they found it in a band of cross-burning hoods who leave James for dead.

❑ **DIAMONDBACK #4: Game of Chance**   0-515-12806-6
Dex Yancey would do anything for three thousand dollars—even pose as a hitman. But pulling the trigger is another story. Especially when the intended victim is a rich beauty with plans of her own for Dex. And she's bartering with something more precious than gold.

❑ **DIAMONDBACK #5: Dead Man's Hand**   0-515-12888-0
After defending a woman's honor, Dex's friend ends up behind bars. And Dex must play all his cards close to the vest to save his friend—when the stakes are raised to life or death.

❑ **DIAMONDBACK #6: Made in Spades**   0-515-12955-0
Dex Yancey introduces a British gentleman to some Southern hospitality—con man style...

To Order Call:
1-800-788-6262

(Ad # B259)

JAKE LOGAN
TODAY'S HOTTEST ACTION WESTERN!

☐ SLOCUM AND THE WOLF HUNT #237   0-515-12413-3
☐ SLOCUM AND THE BARONESS #238   0-515-12436-2
☐ SLOCUM AND THE COMANCHE PRINCESS #239   0-515-12449-4
☐ SLOCUM AND THE LIVE OAK BOYS #240   0-515-12467-2
☐ SLOCUM AND THE BIG THREE #241   0-515-12484-2
☐ SLOCUM AT SCORPION BEND #242   0-515-12510-5
☐ SLOCUM AND THE BUFFALO HUNTER #243   0-515-12518-0
☐ SLOCUM AND THE YELLOW ROSE OF TEXAS #244 0-515-12532-6
☐ SLOCUM AND THE LADY FROM ABILENE #245   0-515-12555-5
☐ SLOCUM GIANT: SLOCUM AND THE THREE WIVES 0-515-12569-5
☐ SLOCUM AND THE CATTLE KING #246   0-515-12571-7
☐ SLOCUM #247: DEAD MAN'S SPURS   0-515-12613-6
☐ SLOCUM #248: SHOWDOWN AT SHILOH   0-515-12659-4
☐ SLOCUM AND THE KETCHEM GANG #249   0-515-12686-1
☐ SLOCUM AND THE JERSEY LILY #250   0-515-12706-X
☐ SLOCUM AND THE GAMBLER'S WOMAN #251   0-515-12733-7
☐ SLOCUM AND THE GUNRUNNERS #252   0-515-12754-X
☐ SLOCUM AND THE NEBRASKA STORM #253   0-515-12769-8
☐ SLOCUM #254: SLOCUM'S CLOSE CALL   0-515-12789-2
☐ SLOCUM AND THE UNDERTAKER #255   0-515-12807-4
☐ SLOCUM AND THE POMO CHIEF #256   0-515-12838-4
☐ SLOCUM AND THE MOUNTAIN SPIRIT #257   0-515-12871-6
☐ SLOCUM #258 SLOCUM'S PARTNER   0-515-12889-9
☐ SLOCUM #259 SLOCUM AND WILD BILL'S LADY 0-515-12909-7
☐ SLOCUM #260: SLOCUM AND THE GILA RANGERS 0-515-12931-3
☐ SLOCUM #261: SLOCUM AND THE SENORITA   0-515-12956-9
☐ SLOCUM #262: SLOCUM AND THE AMBUSH TRAIL 0-515-12976-3
☐ SLOCUM # 263: SHOWDOWN IN TEXAS   0-515-13000-1
☐ SLOCUM #264: SLOCUM AND THE LAKOTA LADY 0-515-13017-6
☐ SLOCUM #265: SLOCUM AND THE RICH MAN'S SON 0-515-13029-X
☐ SLOCUM #266:SLOCUM AND THE BLUE-EYED HOSTAGE
                                           0-515-13045-1
☐ SLOCUM #267: SLOCUM'S SIDEKICK   0-515-13056-7
☐ SLOCUM #268: SLOCUM AND THE HIRED GUN   0-515-13064-8

TO ORDER CALL:

1-800-788-6262

(Ad # B110)